Penguin Books

Uphill Runner

James McQueen was born in 1934 in Ulverstone, Tasmania. He started writing in 1975 at the age of forty, and has been writing full-time since 1977. His published works include two novels (*A Just Equinox* and *Hook's Mountain*), two collections of short stories (*The Electric Beach* and *The Escape Machine*), a children's novel (*Escape to Danger*), and *The Franklin — Not Just a River* (non-fiction).

He has won many competitions for his fiction, including the State of Victoria short story competition (1978, 1979), the Air New Zealand P.E.N. short story award (1978, 1979) and the Henry Lawson Prose Award (1979, 1982).

He lives in Nabowla, Tasmania.

Also by the author

The Electric Beach (stories) 1978
Escape to Danger (children's novel) 1979
A Just Equinox (novel) 1980
The Escape Machine (stories) 1981
Hook's Mountain (novel) 1982
The Franklin — Not Just a River (non-fiction) 1983

Uphill Runner

James McQueen

Penguin Books
Published with the assistance
of the Literature Board
of the Australia Council

... for Lorelle, with love

Penguin Books Australia Ltd,
487 Maroondah Highway, P.O. Box 257
Ringwood, Victoria, 3134, Australia
Penguin Books Ltd,
Harmondsworth, Middlesex, England
Penguin Books,
40 West 23rd Street, New York, N.Y. 10010, U.S.A.
Penguin Books Canada Ltd,
2801 John Street, Markham, Ontario, Canada
Penguin Books (N.Z.) Ltd,
182-190 Wairau Road, Auckland 10, New Zealand

First published by Penguin Books Australia, 1984

Collection Copyright © James McQueen, 1984

Typeset in Concorde by Dovatype, Melbourne.
Made and printed in Australia by
The Dominion Press-Hedges & Bell, Victoria

McQueen, James, 1934-.
Uphill Runner.

ISBN 014 007007 9.

I. Title

A 823'.3

Contents

The Blue Crane

She came out into the silver morning and stood for a moment looking down towards the flats by the creek. The still dark shapes of the plovers dotted the pale stubble. Beyond them the ti-trees along the creek were no more than vague shadows in the slow-drifting skeins of mist. On the distant ridge the tall ring-barked gums held their stark claws against the pale sky.

It took her half an hour to walk round the paddocks, to check on her own cows and the ones on agistment. Even in the bitter frosts of winter and in the great gales of the equinoxes she never missed her morning patrols. It seemed to her that they were the most important part of her day; a time between sleep and the dull round of work when she could renew her precarious foothold on the shaky rungs of her hopes. For that short half-hour in the mornings she could set aside for a little time the problems of a twenty-three-year-old girl, alone, attempting to farm seventy acres and still earn enough by teaching to meet the interest payments and the promissory notes; the problems of no working dogs, of trespassers and spotlighters; of suspicious neighbours, of gossip and peeping toms.

She was almost past the creek pastures when she saw the first grey-blue shape, immobile, elegant, beyond the plovers. And she stopped, counted. There were three of them, and soon there would be more. Each autumn the blue cranes came, stayed a while, moved on. And each time for the past three seasons she had watched them in the autumn mornings; tall pearly birds that never moved far from the creek flats until the day came for them to continue their journey. She knew that they were really white-faced herons, and not cranes at all; but everyone called them cranes, and somehow it seemed to make them even more magical, more poetical, more graceful. She wondered if this year she might be lucky enough to find one of the rare breeding pairs.

But the sun was mounting implacably higher, and the mist was thinning, and soon it would be time to drive the ten miles to the school. She hurried on to check the agisted cows.

One was down, lying by the barn. She walked closer, tried to persuade the cow to its feet. Like all the rest, it was with calf. The barren ones had been sold as choppers at the end of the summer.

For a moment she stood irresolute, the black cow looking up at her with moist melancholy eyes. There was nothing really that she could do, so she turned away, hurrying to make up the lost minutes.

The mist was gone now, and with it most of the morning's enchantment.

At the first recess she rang Harry, the cow's owner, from the school office.

'Sure she can't get up?' He sounded doubtful.

'Pretty sure,' she said, knowing that he suspected her expertise. 'I did try.'

'All right,' he said, reluctantly. 'I'll come round tonight. I'll bring the vet ...'

The bell was ringing, and she had missed her cup of tea.

They turned away from the vet's back as he bent over the cow. The sun was low in the sky, basting the streaks of fatty cloud that hung above the ridge.

'Come on,' she said, 'I'll make you a cup of tea.'

Harry was scowling, his square red face set in lines of permanent depression by the vicissitudes of stock and seasons, banks and brucellosis. 'Always bloody something,' he said. 'She's too fat, she's got too much condition on, everything at the wrong time.'

'Never mind,' she said, because she liked Harry well enough, 'perhaps it's not too serious.'

'Bloody calving paralysis,' he said. 'I'll bet.'

'Wait,' she said, leading him into the kitchen, 'wait and see what the vet says.'

He drained his cup. 'I'd better go and see what's going on.'

'I'll take him a cup of tea.'

He waited while she poured it.

The vet was standing up, wiping his hands, the fine red hairs on his forearms touched with gold by the lowering sun. He took the cup, drank thirstily.

'Thanks.' He handed back the cup, turned to Harry, who was regarding the cow morosely. 'Not so good,' said the vet. 'She's got a nerve pinched, I think. I tried to bring her on, but no go. You can put the clamps on your tractor, if you like, try and stand her up. But it won't do any good ...'

'Sure?'

'Sure.'

Harry spat. 'All right. I'll ring Jock to come and take her away.'

Jock, she knew, was the man who destroyed sick and injured cows, disposed of the carcases.

The two men turned and walked towards the vet's car. She followed them. The words were out before she even thought. 'Harry — leave her here, won't you? I'll look after her. I'm sure she'll get better ...'

Harry paused, turned and looked at her for a moment. He seemed puzzled. 'Well,' he said, 'all right ... if that's what you want.'

He got into the car, shaking his head. The vet looked at him, then started the engine.

When they had gone she walked back to the barn, picked up an armful of hay. She carried it out to the cow, dropped it by the beast's head. For a moment she stood staring down towards the darkening creek. There were two more cranes, now, still and silent in the twilight.

On the second night the frosts came, early and hard. Each evening after that, feeling the steely chill that came with sunset, she covered the cow with an old horse-rug and dry sacks. The cow never moved, but mooed a little, plaintively. She would shake her head, shivering, and go back to the warm house.

Each morning she rushed through her chores, spent more and more time with the sick cow. She tried to feed it, keep it warm, clean it as best she could. But each day the cow grew visibly weaker. A small chill whisper of something almost like despair would touch her each time she looked down at the cow, and she would wonder again what had prompted her to interfere, to try and save the beast. It would have been different, explicable, had there been anything of sentimentality in her action; but she was a farmer's daughter, and a farmer herself, and a beast was a beast and no more. All the same, she knew that she could not have acted differently.

As the cow had come to occupy more and more of her time in the mornings, so she had almost stopped watching the cranes. It was only on the fourth morning she noticed that one of them had moved away from the small group by the creek and stood now almost halfway up the paddock's slope, clearly visible from the barn. She thought no more of it, but set to cleaning the cow's smeared hindquarters.

But that evening it seemed to her that the bird had moved appreciably close. On the following morning there was no doubt. There was a heavy fog, but the tall shape of the bird was clearly visible, no more than twenty paces from the cow. It did not move as she approached, and it was still there when she left.

That evening the bird was no more than six feet from the cow. It moved reluctantly back as she approached, but drew closer again when she returned to the house. She looked out once more, before she went to bed, and in the clear starlight saw the dark birdshape sentry-still beside the cow's head.

For the next few days the bird did not seem to move at all, except to retreat a little at her approach. There seemed no rational explanation for its vigil; it was almost as if the two of them, bird and beast, were bound together by some strong filament of animal spirit that transcended the mere armatures of form and purpose.

The cow grew steadily weaker.

And still the bird watched.

She found that now she watched the bird more often than she watched the cow.

One afternoon she came home from school and went straight to the cow. The bird now hardly moved at her approach. The cow was very thin and weak. She knelt down, felt the staring coat. Then saw the maggots under the slimed hindquarters. And she knew that the cow was going to die.

On her way back to the house she felt the tears begin to form in her eye-corners, and the beginnings of a hard ache in her throat. She went to the telephone and called Jock.

He could not come till the next morning, and she thought that by then it would not matter anyway. She went back to the barn, covered the cow for the night.

When she came out of the house the next morning the

sun was shining brightly, and only along the creek bed a thick bank of mist still hugged the contours of the land. She could not see the cranes by the creek. And thought: surely it's too soon for them to be gone ...

Then she turned, and saw the lone crane, sleek and pearly, by the cow's head. And she saw, too, that there was no steam rising from the horse-rug that covered the cow; and she knew that it was finally dead, and had been dead for hours.

Yet the crane still waited, unreleased.

But as she walked slowly towards the barn the bird stirred a little. And as she drew nearer it took a few small steps towards the creek and, as if freed by her coming, spread its great wings and took flight. It flew low over the dewy stubble, beating its slow way towards the mist-bank by the creek. And soon it began to fade into the mist, grey into grey, its slim outline dissolving slowly to a faint shadow. Then it was gone, and the morning lay bright and still, and there was nothing for her to see except the wooded tops of the far hills that rose like small dark thunderheads above the mist.

A Matter of Self Respect

When the tin price stirred, edged up a little, there must have been a few mutterings in the board room, a flurry of those familiar blue memos fluttering downward to the operations offices; a quick search of the lease files, reassessments, rapid cost-benefit analyses in the rarified atmosphere of the cost accounting surgeries.

Then, when the LME price shot up almost overnight, when the buffer stock manager started selling frantically, when production quotas were lifted, there must have been some real nail-biting. Because we had really very little on the list. And gambling on copper futures, coal contangos, fighting off the conservationists to keep the rutile flowing — well, that's one thing; but missing out on a tin boom was another altogether.

So, somewhere on the seventeenth floor of the concrete castle on Circular Quay, the geologists punted on their best — their only — bet.

And the next thing I knew I was stuck on that bloody island, with the bits and pieces of a fifty-year-old mill, some quickly fudged-up flow charts, a couple of dozers, and an office in a battered old WOWIC donga.

There was a crew, of course, stores, reagents, everything that we could cram on the fortnightly ketch. Not much, not enough. But that was it. And I was the bunny. No acceptable excuses for failure when the price of tin was climbing every day. It was midsummer, and good sweating weather;

but I'd sweat a little bit more every time I'd open a week-old *Financial Review* and see the climbing line on the graph.

It was really a simple enough operation. Opencast, with plenty of lode ore close to the surface. It ran deep, with up to 3 per cent cassiterite. But it was going to take time to get down to it, and anyway, we didn't have a flotation plant built to take out the sulphides. So the core of the operation, in the short term, was the five hundred acres of weathered gossan right on the surface. It was assaying 7 per cent, and we didn't need flotation — crush it, and the vanners and tables we'd brought in would concentrate it. All pretty makeshift, but I had a good metallurgist and a rough, hard-working crew. Plenty of overtime, I ran them ragged. There was nothing else to do on the island, anyway. A single pub thirty miles away and about six females, all tucked away on the soldier-settler farms.

By the end of the first month we were making good time on the construction side, and I'd stopped fretting over the critical path chart. But getting the gossan stripped and refined was the problem. We had a fortnightly quota — all the old ship would carry — and it was worth $125,000. What the accountants call generating a cash flow. The old mill was OK, but I had only two dozers, and with downtime for maintenance the stockpile was always too low for comfort, hardly any margin at all.

Just two dozers, and two drivers.

Then, suddenly, two dozers and one driver.

Marek — the one they called the Beast — got his arm broken in a Saturday-night tangle with a couple of local fishermen. That left only the Kiwi.

On the Monday I tried out a couple of the mechanics, but they were hopeless — they handled the Cats with all the finesse of a pig with a musket. The Kiwi was dragging his black arse as hard as he could go, but by the end of the day the stockpile was a good twenty tons smaller.

The ship had just left, we had no airstrip, so the earlie. time I could expect a replacement operator was a fortnight away.

I was in a pretty foul mood that night. Sitting under the hissing white glare of a Tilley lamp — we had a generator, but it had only enough capacity to run the machinery — I made my calculations. And started to feel awfully cold under all the sweat. We were going to run out of ore very soon. Not *my* fault; but as I said, no excuses accepted. Not that they'd say anything of course, but there'd be a black mark on the record. And I'm too old to be able to afford black marks.

In the end I turned in, worrying. I woke in the morning still worrying.

After breakfast I went into the site clerk's tent and sat in one of the canvas chairs. The temperature was 32° already.

'Listen, Sandy,' I said. 'Where do we find a gun operator on this bloody island? In a hurry?'

Sandy finished pencilling a timesheet, sat back and looked at me. He was young, tall, a bit lazy. One of the locals. I didn't mind the lazy part — he knew the island, and anyway I was always close enough to keep an eye on him. Besides, you always need *one* lazy man on the job to find the easy way of doing things. Only one, though.

He scratched the fair bristles on his chin. 'Well,' he said, 'maybe one of the farmers'd give you a hand for a few days...'

'Any good?'

'No.'

'Then that's a bloody lot of help.'

Then I noticed him looking a bit thoughtful.

'What is it?'

'Oh,' he said, 'you might try the Ag Bank — they've got half a dozen machines on the go...'

'Who do I see?'

'Arthur Warren's the trump,' he said. 'You'll find him up near Egg Lagoon, I reckon.'

'Come on,' I said, 'you can introduce me.'

It was fifty miles over bad roads, but we did it in an hour, ploughing the battered Toyota through the thick white dust. After a while it seemed as thick inside the cab as it was outside. Even the bugs didn't seem able to penetrate it.

As we racketed past the eight or nine buildings that made up the town I shouted into Sandy's ear. 'What about a case of whisky? Sweeten him up?'

Sandy laughed, gave a quick sly grin. 'Don't reckon — he's a strict Methodist, never touches it ...'

That was that.

When we got to Egg Lagoon we were coated in a kind of pale mud composed of white dust and sweat, and Warren was nowhere in sight. It took another half hour of blundering round bush tracks before we found him. He was perched on the top of a wind-rowed log-pile, watching the orange machines crawling like orange beetles through the heat haze of the stripped plain. We clambered up and stood beside him.

Sandy introduced me, and I gave him the story. As I talked I watched him carefully. He was thin, dark, with a face as brown and angular — and as expressive — as adzed teak. He looked at me once as I talked, then turned his head back to watch the machines as if he was afraid that one of them might escape. When I'd finished, he gave me his answer.

'No,' he said.

I looked at him for a moment, then at Sandy. Sandy shrugged, shook his head. I could see it was pointless to argue. After all, I suppose he had his own quotas. We were back at the bottom of the log-pile when Warren spoke again.

'You might try Blue,' he said. 'If you can find him,
should be just about ready ...'

'Who's Blue?' I asked.

'Sandy knows,' he said. 'If you can get him to the missus
today, you can probably have him the day after tomorrow.'
He risked one quick look down at us. 'Just for a week, then
I'll need him.'

'Well,' I said to Sandy when we were back at the Toyota,
'who's this Blue? What's it all about?'

He grinned a bit sheepishly. 'Tell the truth I didn't think
of him before. Thought he was still on the job.'

'Who *is* he?'

'He's the best dozer driver on the island.'

'Why isn't he on the job, then?'

'Oh,' said Sandy, 'he gets on the piss occasionally, just
buggers off ...'

'And Warren always takes him back?'

'Of course,' said Sandy. 'I told you, he's the best on the
island. Worth about five of the rest of them.'

'Come on, then,' I said. 'Let's find this bloody marvel.'

But I'm too old to believe in miracles, and I didn't have
much hope of one then.

It took us a couple of hours to track him down. First, the
hotel. No, they hadn't seen him since he'd been barred a
couple weeks ago.

'We'll try the boongs,' said Sandy. By then the temperature was pushing forty.

Half a mile out of town we turned down a narrow track
through the thin scrub and drove on until we came to a
creek bed. The water in the channel was a dark scummy
trickle. Flies buzzed round three or four kerosene-tin
humpies and over a few middens I didn't care to look too
closely at. Under the sparse shade of a twisted she-oak sat
two young Aborigines, dressed in ragged shorts and

singlets, passing a wine bottle back and forth. We pulled up under their disinterested stare. Sandy got out and went over, spoke briefly to them. In a minute or so he came back.

'Well,' he said, 'he's not here — wore out his welcome a week back.'

I was tired, thirsty, short-tempered. Only the thought of the dwindling stockpile kept me going. 'All right,' I said, 'where to now?'

'We'd better start looking in the culverts,' said Sandy. 'They're usually the next stop.'

I'd never realized there were so many culverts on the island. I swear we stopped and looked under every one. It seemed to go on for hours. And still no Blue.

Then Sandy spotted the stack of four-foot concrete pipes lying in the shade a hundred yards back from the road. We trudged wearily over the dry crumbling soil, threading our way between the gaunt blackboys, native heath prickling our bare legs.

We found him in the third pipe. I smelt him before I saw him.

The inside of the pipe was dark after the glare outside, and for a moment I couldn't see a thing. But the stink ...

'A bit ripe, eh?' said Sandy.

I shook my head in disgust. We crawled in and dragged him out. Blue. I had a good look at him as he lay, semi-comatose, mumbling uneasily. About thirty-five, short, wiry, gingery hair, freckles. Old jeans, ragged workshirt, bare feet. His lips were dry, cracked and blackened, white-scummed at the corners. He was indescribably filthy, smeared and fouled. The stink of urine, vomit, stale sweat, methylated spirits.

I sighed. I really *did* feel sorry for him. But it was a day wasted, and still I had my own problem. 'Come on,' I said, 'we'd better get him to the doctor.'

Sandy shook his head. 'Mrs Warren'll fix him up.'

'You've got to be joking — he's half dead.'

'She'll fix him up …'

So we dragged him to the Toyota, heaved him into the back. I went back to the pipe to collect his belongings. There wasn't much there. A scattering of empty bottles — mostly methylated spirits — a carton containing a dirty shirt, a few paperback books, shaving gear, a pair of sandshoes, a clutter of odds and ends. I took the carton and tossed it into the Toyota.

In town we parked outside the Warrens' house, a surprisingly neat white weatherboard cottage next to the post office. We carried Blue in through the back gate.

A plump middle-aged lady was pegging out the washing. Pink face, wire-rimmed specs, a grey bun. She saw us coming and dropped the peg bag. I swear she was clucking.

'In there,' she said, leading us towards a sleepout by the back door. Inside, she ignored us, concentrated on Blue. We stood round for a few minutes, but she took no more notice of us. We went out, leaving her washing his face, dragging off the filthy shirt.

'Won't see *him* on his feet under a week,' I said as we drove off.

'Want to bet?' asked Sandy.

I ignored him, thinking of that bloody stockpile and the wasted day.

The next morning I took a machine myself, trying to keep up with the Kiwi. But it was no good. That night, I decided I'd have to close the mill for the rest of the week. Then, angry and sullen, I shared a bottle of whisky with the Kiwi, and went to bed still unhappy, and drunk to boot.

When I walked into Sandy's tent next morning, hung-over and snappish, the first person I saw was Blue, standing by Sandy's desk. I stopped and blinked at him.

He was clean, dressed in fresh dungarees and singlet.

And sober. Far from healthy, very red round the eyes and with a touch of the shakes, but definitely sober. And *there*.

'They tell me you want a man,' he said. His voice was as shaky as his hands, but he looked me right in the eye.

'Are you up to it?' I said. 'I don't want one of my machines scrambled.'

'She'll be right,' he said. And before I knew it he was out of the tent, gone. A couple of minutes later I heard the cough and stutter of an engine as he started one of the D8s. I crossed my fingers and walked out to watch.

I stood there for a few minutes, then I went back inside and dragged out a chair. Just sat watching. I didn't move for more than an hour. Even the Kiwi hauled in to an idle once for a look.

I've never seen anything like it. He was a gun, all right, Blue. He used that big blade the way a surgeon uses a scalpel. No waste motion, no second runs. He peeled that gossan from the ground the way you'd peel an orange. It was a strange machine, new ground, he was ill enough to be in hospital — but he was taking a slice that didn't leave half an inch of waste. And leaving the Kiwi for dead. A real gun.

At smoko he climbed down, took a long drink of water from the bag, spewed, drank again, and climbed back into the seat.

'How did she do it?' I asked Sandy.

He looked up from his tonnage sheets. 'Christ knows. Soup, herbs, orange juice ... prayer, for all I know.'

I shook my head. I still couldn't really believe it.

I caught sight of the carton I'd rescued from the pipe. It was in the corner where I'd thrown it two days before. We'd forgotten to leave it at the Warrens. I picked it up, dropped it on the desk. 'Better give him this. And see if he wants a sub ...'

Then something in the box caught my eye. Something

white and clean in the middle of all the grubby clutter. I picked it out and held it up. It was a lamp mantle, a Tilley-lamp mantle, brand new, still in its glassine pack. I poked down into the carton. There were more. I raked them out, laid them in a line on Sandy's desk. There were nine of them; all new, virgin, snow-white.

What the hell was he doing with nine brand-new lamp mantles? Nine! There hadn't even been a lamp in the pipe, only a guttered candle-end.

I looked at Sandy. 'What the bloody hell was he doing with these? *Nine* of them! Bloody lamp mantles!'

For the first time I saw something in Sandy's face that I'd never noticed before. A kind of gentleness.

'Look,' he said, 'if you were Blue — crook with the grog — living in that bloody pipe — and if you had to wake up every morning, walk into town and front up to that old bitch at the shop, ask for a bottle of metho — what would *you* do?'

I still didn't get it. 'What do you mean?'

'You saw how he was. How bloody low. Can't get much lower, can you? But he had to have *something* to hang onto, see? Couldn't just walk in and buy a bottle of metho, right? So he pretended he wanted it to prime a Tilley. And every time he bought a bottle, he bought a lamp mantle too. Just pretending. *She* knew, of course, everyone knew. But he had to have *something*, didn't he?'

I walked out of the tent into the blinding sunlight. Blue's machine was roaring a hundred yards away, and I could hear the rumble as he pushed up the mound of gossan. I knew it was a delight to see, the way he was working, something good and clean and sharp, a kind of rightness to it as keen and true as a knife.

But I couldn't look at him just then. For some reason — I still don't know why — I felt suddenly ashamed.

Funeral at Tautira

It would have been all right if we'd made it back to the museum in time, if she hadn't wanted to stop and watch them putting up a big thatched roof at Pueu. It looked like a church of some kind, full of magic geodesic angles like a hip-roofed pagoda, but they were putting thatch on the roof instead of tile or colourbond or whatever. Half a dozen of them, stripped to the waist, up there on the steep rafters laying the palm fronds. It wasn't even good thatching — they were just twisting the leaflets back over the spines, laying them straight, not plaiting them. Lazy man's thatch, it's bloody everywhere in Tahiti. She wanted to watch, though, and made me stop the car; got out and lay in the sun in the long grass by the side of the road. I stayed in the car smoking. Knowing there'd be trouble, because the shithouse at the Gauguin Museum was the only safe place we'd found that day, and we'd be late getting back there, and she'd be well into the itches by then.

Well, holidays …

Rarotonga was OK. The form they gave us to fill in on the plane scared shit out of her. It was the size of a brummy prospectus, with a great coat of arms on the front, and you had to declare just about everything you'd ever owned, where you got it, how much you paid for it; how many secondhand bicycles you were importing, how many wheeled toys, everything short of your Tek toothbrush.

That got her nervous. But when it came to the point the Customs were OK. They went through us, but all they seemed worried about was the duty-free grog allowance. They hardly looked at us, really. She had the needle in her hair, the eyedropper in her toilet bag, and the smack up her snatch tied to a Tampax string. A teaspoon you can find anywhere, and I had a couple of ties in my luggage.

A nice quiet little motel, no hassles. Ten days of bliss. I thought that probably she might just as well have stayed at home. But then she *did* seem to enjoy it once we were there, the reef, the sea everywhere, and all the new colours seemed to turn her on.

And when she's right, she's right, and I wouldn't want to be with anyone else. And sometimes she says she wants to get straight and I know she means it.

After a while she'd had enough of the thatching, so she climbed back into the car and I drove on down the narrow blacktop to Tautira. It was the end of the road, and nothing to see. Just another crappy village, the road petering out, a scruffy little beach. But Tautira was where all the great canoe-men were supposed to come from, the ones that won all the big July races every year in Papeete. So we had to go and see it.

There was a kind of open paddock covered with thin grass and, off to one side, a tight neat clean little *Mairie* with the glorious flag of France hanging outside like a limp dick. Down by the water we could see a big open shelter with this enormous double-hulled canoe under it, on rollers. We went down to look at it. It must have been a hundred feet long, and so big they must have needed half the population of the bloody peninsula to paddle it. It was painted all over in a kind of dull rusty red, and the carved ends curved up way above our heads.

She wanted to know how old it was. I reckoned at least a hundred years. I was going to go back and ask at the

Mairie, but then I heard the raw scream of a chain saw, and looked along the beach. There were three young coconuts in shorts and straw hats making little canoes.

I walked over. At least they were making them properly, using real logs, marking out the contours in sections, getting the curves right, hollowing out the centres. Not like the lazy buggers in the Cook Islands with their ramshackle plywood boxes tied together with bits of wire and old rope.

My French is pretty awful, and the kids were a surly bunch, but after they talked it over for a while they agreed to tell me.

I went back to where she was standing and said, 'Twenty years.'

'Is that all?'

'What do you expect? This is bloody Tahiti. Look at the motel — if anything they build here sees the year out you're lucky.'

I looked at my watch again. It was about twenty miles back to the museum. She was still in pretty fair shape, but I noticed that she'd started to scratch a bit. With some of them it's runny noses, the wheezes, watery eyes. With her it was scratching and, later, sneezes. So I got her into the car, turned it round and headed back the way we'd come.

And that's when we got mixed up in the bloody funeral.

Until we'd met Peter we'd planned on going straight back to Auckland. Then one day we'd been down on the rocks near Avarua looking at the wreck of the old *Yankee*, and when we came up again past the public lavatories into the main drag there he'd been, sitting on a Honda scooter with a blond bird rubbing herself up against him on the pillion. He'd just brought a yacht in from Sydney, and he was flying on to Tahiti, he said. Why not come? he said, Tahiti's fun.

So we decided — she did — that we'd go. Normally we

wouldn't even have considered it, French Customs and no connections and all that. But Peter knew all about us, and he said he'd guarantee she'd connect, all we had to do was get there. So we flew on with him, on the same flight. He was picking up another yacht at Papeete, he said, sailing it north to the Marquesas, then to L.A.

She got very nervous at Faaa — she was still holding. Running low, but holding. I suppose really that we were safe enough. She looks pretty straight — neat, clean, well-groomed. But she was nervous, all the same, by the time we'd got through immigration. All those blank-faced French security men with big black pistols in their belts. And at Customs they were really going through a China-man in front of us. We just stood there waiting. But after a couple of minutes, while his mate was still digging through the Chinaman's undies, this plump little charac-ter in a flowered shirt just came over and said to us, Do you have any fruit? We shook our heads and he waved us straight through. Fucking fruit ...

Peter went off on his own, he had to find his crew, and he didn't even know if the yacht had docked yet. So we hired a car and found a motel room at the edge of town. The first night we went round the spots. Pretty grotty. But the food was good. And one or two of the high-class whores looked all right. To tell the truth, I was a bit tempted, because she's never interested much nowadays.

I woke up in the morning to see her sitting on the end of the bed, shooting up, digging for a vein in her leg. She likes to keep her arms clean. It means she always has to wear slacks, but she reckons it's worth it. Anyway, that was it, the end of the stash, the last fix.

So I knew we'd have to find Peter.

Fucking holidays ...

The worst of it was that neither of us could remember the name of the boat. She'd thought I'd remember, and I'd thought she would. It was only about 7.30, but we drove down to the yacht basin to start looking. No good trying to go back to sleep, anyway; every bugger in Tahiti seems to get up at 5 o'clock, and if he's not roaring round on a scooter or on one of those homemade hurdygurdy buses, then he's hammering shit out of a piece of sheet-iron outside your window.

I must say it was nice down by the water. All the hills were a kind of greeny gold, and the water was so smooth you could see the reflections of the boats just like in a mirror. And Moorea, only ten miles away; after one look at it, the mountains, the shape of it, something, I don't know, I wanted to go there. But we couldn't, of course.

The yachts were all tied up stern to the dock opposite the wide boulevard that ran right round the bay, and we walked along in the early sunlight looking at them. There were all kinds — an ancient black hulk of a Danish thing that might have been a hundred years old, sleek ocean racers, floating gin palaces, little thirty-footers you'd swear couldn't have made it across the harbour but had names like *Southampton, Le Havre, Boston,* on their transoms. It was a good time, she was high and happy, and we held hands as we walked along, swinging our arms, just like we used to.

And it all seemed to be working out OK. Because halfway along the dock we found the boat. It was a ripper. About fifty feet, a tall sloop with nice lines and no frills, that look of order and brightness that means a real boat that goes places. Everything clean and shiny, like a good gun. And worth Christ knows how much. Peter was sitting in the well-deck in the sun, stripped to his shorts, drinking coffee with a nice-looking middle-aged lady with sun-bleached hair.

We didn't get invited aboard. Maybe they were getting ready for the day's work, or maybe the lady was getting ready to screw Peter. But they were nice enough, friendly, and Peter told us where to meet him that night.

The first sign of the funeral that I saw was a little convoy of beat-up cars and vans bumping out onto the road ahead of us through a gap in the technicolour hedge. Beautiful luxuriant foliage ... yeah, looks like someone's chundered a mixture of hot dogs and fruit salad all over the landscape.

So there were all these cars with coconuts all dressed up in white, masses of flowers everywhere. And a very alert young copper in trim khaki with red tabs and capband and a big pistol in his belt. Oh shit, I thought, oh shit, on a bloody twelve-foot blacktop and we have to get pulled up...

But he took no more notice of us, once I'd pulled in to the side of the road. He turned and beckoned some more of them through the hedge. And then this marvellous colourful genuine bloody Tahitian hearse rolled out onto the road. It was an open thirty-hundredweight, packed with coconuts sitting on benches along the sides, and a yellow coffin on the floor between their knees. Everything stacked high with frangipani and hibiscus and Christ knows what. It bumped out onto the road, the coffin jerking around, the mourners hanging on like barnacles. Then it set off, going our way, at about forty miles an hour.

More beat-up cars and trucks, even a motorbike or two, dribbled out of gaps and gateways onto the road and followed the hearse. Then I heard a chorus of beepings from behind, looked in the mirror, and there were more of them; a rusty Fiat, a two-horse Citroen, a Ford ute, a rusty Mercedes bus, all honking at me to get moving. And the copper waving at me to shove off.

So we joined the funeral.

We waited till nearly 11 o'clock in this bloody floating bar. A kind of Chinese junk, all black and red, with a real gangplank and all. Her last fix had been early in the morning, and she was pretty wasted by the time we got there. Just

sat there crumbling cigarettes, sipping orange juice, sucking lollies, never taking her eyes off the door.

Then Peter came in, looked round, saw us.

She'd always been friendly with Peter, we all went a long
way back together. But that night she snarled at him, a
kind of whispered scream. '*Where is it?*'

I bought Peter a drink, and he sat down. 'Don't worry,'
he said to her. 'Everything's fine. Just cool it a bit …'

So she sat quietly for a while. But I knew that her nerves
were strung as tight as guitar strings.

After a few minutes a fat Chinaman came over. He'd
been sitting there all the time, but we'd taken no notice
of him. He talked to Peter in something that wasn't either
French or English.

'He wants his money,' said Peter, and told me how
much. 'Give it to me, I'll pass it on later.'

I gave the notes to Peter. Once the Chinaman saw the
money he started talking again.

'Go back to your car,' said Peter. We'd parked half a mile
away, up near the fishing boats.

'But when do I *get* it?' she said.

'You've got it,' said Peter, and grinned. 'It's taped under
your back bumper. But drive out of the city before you
unstick it, huh?'

I wanted to have another drink with Peter, Christ knew
when we'd see him again. But I didn't even suggest it.

She almost ran back to the car. And there was no waiting till we got out of town. She had her fit with her, and
she disappeared into the filthy shithouse up by the
Moorea boat-dock. When she came back it was all right
again, and we went off to one of the gay bars on the *Rue
des Écoles* for a bit of a giggle.

It was about twelve miles back to Tahiti Nui, another five
or so to the museum. And on that road there was no way

to pass a couple of dozen microbuses and vans, to say nothing of a flat-bed hearse and a copper in a jeep.

So we ground painfully along in first gear.

More and more vehicles straggled out in the first mile or so to join in. I didn't know where the cemetery was — it could have been in Papeete for all I knew — and there wasn't a bloody thing I could do about it.

We must have been about halfway to the isthmus, near Pueu — yes, I remember that bloody thatched church or whatever it was — when she started to sniffle. I knew then that it was all going to start coming down on us.

I didn't look at her, but I could see from the corner of my eye that she was getting edgy, scratching, blowing her nose, twitching about on the seat.

'You'll have to stop,' she said.

'Don't be stupid,' I said. 'How can I stop in the middle of a bloody funeral?'

'I don't care, you'll *have* to stop!'

'I bloody can't!'

Then she started screaming at me. 'Stop, you bastard!' she screeched, the high panic in her voice easily audible to the coconuts in the back of the ute in front of us. 'I need a fix! I need a fucking fix! I need a fix, and I need it fucking *now*!'

We got up early, it was still cool, and she disappeared into the bathroom for her breakfast.

Then we swam in the pool ... well, I swam in the pool, she won't wear a swimsuit of course. But it was a good morning, the sky clear, a nice breeze, the blue outline of Moorea, the drinks cold, the Tahitian waitresses smiling for a change.

Then, about ten, we got in the car and drove off for a trip round the island. We started clockwise, round the top and down the east coast. Had coffee at Faaone, got lost on the backroads near the turn off to Tahiti Iti, then decided we'd better see the Gauguin Museum in case it was closed by the time we got back.

It was good there, cool and shady, the long white buildings, the bare Japanese-looking gardens, the dimness inside. It was almost deserted. So we spent an hour looking at the old diaries and photographs, the reproductions, the wood carvings. The only thing that gave me the shits, all the screeds were so polite about the poor old bastard. Never a word about the pox or anything like that. Still it was good. Then I went for a leak, and when I came out she was nowhere in sight. I stood looking at the carved wooden heads outside the bog doors — there were no notices, just a woman's head outside the ladies, and outside the men's a long hook-jawed profile of the old bugger himself, his great nose pointing at the door. I wondered what he would have thought about it, watching a long parade of pricks going in and out the doorway.

She was taking a long time, but I'd guessed what was happening.

When she came out we walked back to the carpark. She kissed me a couple of times and put her arm round my waist.

There's no road that goes right round the peninsula, so we decided to take the north branch. We'd heard all about the mighty men of Tautira, and thought maybe we'd see them practising with their paddles or something. The bastards are supposed to give up sex for two weeks before the big races, so they must be bloody keen.

I pulled off the road as far as I could, which wasn't far, and before the car had stopped she'd clambered into the back seat and was rooting in her big handbag.

I had the shakes by then. It wasn't just the thought of her shooting up, I'd watched her before, even though I can't stand the thought of sticking a needle in myself. Even to get a splinter out. But the really horrible part is the look in the eyes, because there's no way of hiding *that*. She was using the top of an eski for a table, and I could smell the heating metal, hear the small sounds. And all the time these bloody cars and bikes and trucks were creeping past, I could see the people in them, all solemn brown faces and sad curious eyes, looking down into our car. And I couldn't stop thinking about that fucking policeman up ahead. If he came back. If someone told him and he came back. Getting busted at home is one thing, but the thought of her doing cold turkey in a fucking French gaol and no one wanting to know, that sent the chills through me. I smoked three cigarettes, burned my fingers twice, tried not to look at anyone, tried to pretend it was just an ordinary stop, a piss, a smoke, anything. But, fuck it, I couldn't help it, I was just shit-scared, knowing she was sitting there behind me, shooting up right in the middle of that funeral procession. They'd probably send us off for sacrilege, too.

Then, after a while it got so I didn't care any more. I felt tired and old and shagged out. I wanted to pop a couple of librium — bloody legal, prescription and all — but I wasn't game. Couldn't afford to relax. Left-hand drive, the wrong side of the road, all that. We couldn't afford an accident.

After a while I threw away the last cigarette. 'Are you all right?' I said.

'Yes.' She sounded dopey, happy, and I knew she was on the nod, junked to the eyeballs. Christ knows what kind of flashes she was getting with all those mad colours in the scrub round us, the rainbow paint-jobs on the cars and trucks.

So I started the engine, pulled out, caught up with the tail-end of the funeral. Crawled along for about another five miles until we came to a steep turnoff that led up the hill to the left. The map said it went to somewhere called Toahotu. The copper was standing in the middle of the road, directing the traffic. I flicked the right-hand blinkers and he waved us past. I looked straight ahead, hoping he wouldn't wonder what the hell she was doing in the back seat on her own.

But nothing happened.

I turned left onto the road that led through Papeari and up the west coast to Papeete. No need to stop now at the museum, so I kept right on.

A little way along the road we passed a fat brown man, half naked, squatting motionless with a long string of fish he'd caught. Waiting for someone to buy them, I suppose. The fish were the same bloody outlandish colours as the shrubs and flowers. Worse. Orange and pink and metallic blue and saffron and greeny-black. She wanted to stop and look at them, but I kept going. The sun was low in the sky now and I was driving right into it, the glare making my head ache. Soon we'd start to meet the great stream of traffic heading south from Papeete. I wasn't looking forward to that. I felt old and weary and I wanted a long drink of gin with plenty of tonic and ice.

She was quiet for a long time. But then, about the time we came in sight of Moorea and the traffic started to charge at us round the bends, she spoke to me, her voice kind of sleepy and a long way away.

'You do love me, don't you?'

'Yes,' I said. 'Yes, I love you.'

It's supposed to be living, but I swear to Christ that sometimes it feels more like fucking dying.

Landfall

Melbourne, Monday
Many thousands of migrants are expected to arrive in Australia
before the end of March ... the Greek steamer *Nea Hellas* is in
the Indian Ocean with 1,527 Balts and Slavs aboard. They are
the biggest single shipload of displaced persons that has left
Europe for any country. The vessel will berth in Melbourne ...
— *Age*, 8 February 1949

In the saloon the bridge game slowly loses momentum,
drifts to a stop. The slack sweating faces of the players,
listless over the greasy cards, pivot in slow time to the
ship's motion. Outside, the slow grey metal of the sea
slides past in a procession of queasy hills and valleys. The
sky, heat-leached, burns from horizon to horizon. Josef's
body, like the others, sways against the slow pendulum of
the ship. They seem locked at the centre of the world, the
sea alone in motion, slipping past at fifteen knots.

Josef watches the faces of his three companions; Kurpinski's — broad, dark, lumpy, eyes slitted and private;
Brodzinski's — square, tight-lipped, the skin beginning to
pale a little under its new tan; Sulikowski's — younger than
the rest, round, pocked, fair.

Brodzinski blinks rapidly, swallows audibly. Sulikowski
watches him earnestly.

'Sir,' he asks, 'Doctor ... are you all right?'

Irritation wells up in Josef, along with incipient nausea.

He is irritated with Sulikowski's open fawning, with Brodzinski's offhand acceptance of it, with his fretting resentment.

Brodzinski stands up, quite pale now and sweating heavily, hurries wordlessly from the table. After a moment Sulikowski rises and follows him.

Go, thinks Josef, go, hold his sacred lawyer's head while he spews sacred lawyer's spew...

Feeling the same sickness rising in his own belly, he closes his eyes. But it is worse that way, and after a moment he opens them again. Seeking distraction, he looks round the saloon. It is almost deserted. Waiters drift idly, lethargic and disinterested. Josef feels a little sorry for them. They have few customers, fewer tips. The seven dollars given to each man at Naples did not last long. At Port Said a little wine, oranges, sandals that fell to pieces in a few days. The waiters, thinks Josef, are like us, displaced; their occupations nullified, abandoned for the present. They wait for their next paying cargo, we for ... what?

I am forty years old, thinks Josef, and I am no longer Hungarian. I am no longer even European, no longer a clerk, a timekeeper, no longer a smuggler of lard and sugar over forbidden frontiers; no longer even a painter of signposts for plump raucous Americans; I am a temporary resident of the Indian Ocean, a non-paying guest on a liner whose owners have been paid ... persuaded? ... blackmailed? ... into carrying me across weeks and oceans. No labels now; no baggage. I carry nothing with me. What I have left behind, not even I know. I am simply, solely, me. Me, and perhaps some kind of bitter and qualified hope. And without suspicion I could not bear even that slight hope...

Josef finds that Kurpinski, too, has left the table, that he is alone again.

The ship ploughs steadily on through the furrows of the sea, fifteen days out of Melbourne.

Melbourne: a city both unpronounceable and incomprehensible. On the train, windows are closed against the hot dust-laden north wind. Then, as the heat inside the carriages builds to an intolerable level, the windows are opened again and the wind gusts in with its alien smells, smells as strange as the bland and featureless city that rattles past outside. Melbourne: it sprawls, uncitylike, a random agglomeration as meaningless as a flaw in a yellowed mirror. Beside the bright hot tracks that lead northward, into the wind, towards Bonegilla, dusty trees thrash aimlessly.

'Doctor,' says Sulikowski, leaning towards Brodzinski, 'would you care to change places … face the engine?'

Brodzinski smiles his placid smile. 'Thank you, no.'

Josef says nothing, stares out the window. He is still a little astonished to find himself travelling with the Poles. At first it was simply the bridge games. But now he stays with them by conscious choice. They seem, somehow, to possess a native strength, a purpose, that he can no longer find in himself, in his own countrymen. Yet they continue to irritate him. Kurpinski's sly self-possession, Sulikowski's innocent sycophancy, Brodzinski's bland complacency. And it is Sulikowski who irritates him most. Sulikowski, who at fifteen graduated from school to Auschwitz, who carries unselfconsciously the indelible blue ciphers on his forearm. Sulikowski, who has married a German woman. Sulikowski, who is unfailingly and unequivocally cheerful, ubiquitously courteous and deferential.

Josef sighs.

The points click hypnotically beneath the wheels, and he closes his eyes against the glare. He has known heat before, the heat of the Hungarian plains in summer. But not heat like this. It has a bitter and unrelenting weight that frightens him.

As the sprawl of the suburbs falls behind and they are drawn out along the bright thread of the rails into the spread of land, Josef sinks back into contemplation of his private arithmetic. The past has become not images, but years, numbers. Four plus three equals seven. And each year the arithmetic extends. The memory of his mother has become a mathematical concept, achieving in his mind the sullen and abstract quality of an equation without logic. Brodzinski too, he knows, has his own personal mathematics, and Josef wonders at the composure of the square face. And he wonders, too, if either of them are any nearer now to a solution, sweating on the crowded rattling train, than they were in the bitter winter of the Austrian camp.

Looking through the frame of the window he finds that he doubts the capacity of this land to provide answers. It is too bare and unresponsive: yellow-dun, stubbled, flat. Heat beats back at the hazed sky from shorn fields. He had imagined that it would possess some exotic exuberance, some luxuriant quality. Instead, burnt fields stretch endlessly towards unguessable distances. He looks round at the faces of the others. And sees in them hints of the same weight of apprehension that drags at his own bones. Like him they are moving into new territories that cannot be avoided or denied; they are pioneers and, like all pioneers, they cannot retreat.

Sulikowski breaks the long silence, speaks to Brodzinski.

'Doctor ... how long before we get there?'

Before Brodzinski can reply Josef flares suddenly, his quick anger stretching the skin tight over his cheekbones and narrow chin.

'Why do you let them call you "Doctor"?' he shouts at Brodzinski. 'Why do you let them? You're not a lawyer any more! You're shit, that's all! Just shit, like the rest of us!'

Brodzinski says nothing. The others avoid Josef's eye, ignore his outburst. And suddenly Josef is afraid, afraid that his rage has disturbed the delicate equilibrium of his

survival. For he has needs, he knows, beyond his own cap-
acities; and, recognizing the nature of these needs, he
despises himself.

So he turns to the window, trembling a little. And he
finds no reassurance there; only the land, harsh and
brutal.

Sulikowski leans forward, smiles a little uncertainly,
touches Josef's knee. Josef bites his lip, stares out into the
glare of the swaying land.

The sun, marching in the colours of the land's dust, swings
slowly overhead, measuring off the hours in shards of
moving shadow that spill across the interior of the rocking
carriage. At last the train begins to lose speed. Wheezing
steam, it slides into a station, rolls finally to a halt. In the
sudden stillness they hear about them the small creakings
of the train at rest. Josef, looking out, deciphers yet
another alien name: Benalla. There is a sudden shouting
from the platform. They stretch their legs, look at each
other, lean from windows. Messages, urgent in half a
dozen languages, are flung the length of the train. They
open doors, step stiffly out onto sticky asphalt. On the
platform long trestle tables are set up, covered with stiff
white cloths. Urns boil, fruit glows in the shade, carved
meats splash the linen like wounds, heat beats down from
the iron parasol of the roof.

After the first anxious rush from the carriages they
stand, mute and embarrassed, in the face of some
uncomprehended constraint. Behind the tables aproned
matrons bustle pointlessly, voices too loud, fingers busy
at nothing. A few official men, suited, hatted, sweating, as
awkward as the travellers themselves, stand on rooted feet
in small groups. At last one of them, red-faced, clench-
fisted, steps forward and makes a brief and inaudible
speech. His duty done, he retires behind the urn and
matrons.

There is no one to respond. But they all move forward, slowly, cautiously, a hungry skirmish line advancing on the tables.

Covers are slipped from jugs and dishes, flies swoop, cups rattle, hands reach for fruit — bananas, oranges, apples, pears — and for rolls stuffed richly with butter, lettuce, tomatoes, meat, meat, meat ...

Josef bites into a roll, and butter, running greasily in the heat, trickles down his chin. He knows that he will face days of constipation, but surrenders all the same. Meat, meat ... it is a temptation not to be resisted. There is no certainty, ever. He takes another roll.

Beside him, Brodzinski squeezes his roll flat, reduces it with rapid nibbles. His false teeth are a bad fit, and he cannot open his mouth too widely. They have not spoken since Josef shouted at him. And now Josef feels the full burden of his own anxiety. Exclusion from the group would mean another start, the beginning of another loneliness, to be borne. And the loss of that purpose which he finds, vicariously, in the Poles. He wipes his lips on the back of his hand and pushes close to the table, seizes two great ripe pears. Returning to Brodzinski, he presents the fruit, offering a choice. Brodzinski, stuffing the last of his roll into his mouth, nods absently and takes a pear.

'God knows what all this will do to my bowels,' says Brodzinski.

'I'm sorry,' says Josef, 'for what I said ...'

Brodzinski, battling with false teeth and pear juice, shakes his head. 'No, no ... you were right. It's good that you spoke.' He pauses. 'It's just that they seem to need ... and I'd never thought of it, but you're right.' He smiles suddenly, his detachment lost in a confusion of clogged teeth and juicy pulp. 'Well, I mean ... we're not shit, not that ... but we have nothing, it's true, not even the past. You were right to speak ...'

Josef says nothing. He is disgusted at the craven and

desperate quality of his own apology. But, all the same, he feels the beginning of a small warmth start in him.

Steam hisses, sharp whistles punctuate the afternoon. They stroll back to the carriage carrying fruit, the last of the rolls. The train moves slowly away from the dimness of the station, out again into the waiting bowl of bright heat. Bloated, comatose, they all slump sleepily as the train rocks northward.

Josef, half-dozing, realizes that he is a little suspicious of the prodigality of the land, of its impersonal generosity, of his own full belly even. I can take nothing, he thinks, in trust, and despise myself because of it. We are all the same, we have lost the capacity to trust. Ourselves, each other, we trust perhaps. A little. Knowledge itself can be a kind of trust. Even transgressions, recognized, comprehended, can be a kind of trust. But with strangers, no …

We are barren, he thinks, his mouth still tasting the richness of the land's meat, his body joggling uneasily on the hot leather of the seat; we are barren … we have mistrusted too many promises …

A Wedding Dress, or Something Bright

She stood on the cracked squares of the sloping concrete yard, her thin figure dappled and windbroken by the moving shadows of the walnut leaves. The bicycle leaned against the flaking white of the shed wall and its alien luminescence seemed to tremble a little, to shimmer in the bright day. Secondhand, refurnished, the minute rust-streaks in the chrome almost invisible, it had cost her $50. Fifty dollars from the meagre fund set aside for the repainting of the old house. But there had been no other way; it was too far to walk, the city's buses ran their uncertain, circuitous routes a long way from her gate and the cost of taxis was impossible. So she made her decision. The high weatherboard walls could wait another year.

At first, she had been tempted, almost, to hope that Arthur might suggest some arrangement. It need not — she had accepted the fact reluctantly — have been clothed in any great formality. She had long abandoned polished forms for the chipped and flawed stones of reality. Still, hope had — almost — tempted her. But, conditioned by the years, she had rejected it, had shut it firmly into the cul-de-sac of her mind reserved for lottery wins, bequests, rate reductions.

She had learned. And in the end had bought the bicycle to prevent the contact, however wavering and ambiguous, from being finally broken.

Her purchase was made with a certain cold resolution,

in the knowledge that she was exposing herself to — embracing even — the cruellest of the city's weather. Not the rains, winds, storms; her fifty-five years had accustomed her to them. She barely noticed now the shifts of the season across her skin. The true weather of the city was an ambience more difficult to meet, face, endure. Its weapons were less kind than the wind and sleet: scorn, indifference, casual and crushing charities; sly laughter at an embattled spinster too old to be accounted, too young to be pensioned, too unskilled to be employed, too alone to befriend. All old and familiar cuts, yet her tissues were not yet deadened to their sting.

And beyond these there lay the ultimate monster of her nightmares — ridicule, a beast she had seen from a distance often enough. The city functioned still on coal gas and she had known those who had found it a better friend than friends, a final salve for the daily lacerations; lacerations to which she was preparing, with a trembling purpose, to expose herself.

Of course she was afraid. The fear lay barbed and deep, past the remedies of reason and will. She had never driven any kind of vehicle since her girlhood when she had learned to ride a rusty bicycle in a quiet country lane. And the thought of the speeding traffic that she must broach on her frail bright machine spiked her with such fear that only her desperate need held panic a fragile moment away.

It was with awe now that she contemplated the casual voyages of the eleven-year-old Michael, who did odd jobs for Arthur, through the city's arteries, crossing and recrossing the network of one-way streets, the impossible complexities of the freeways. She thought of his bicycle; ancient, rusted, the brakes clamped to warped members with scraps of corroded iron, the handlebars bound with strips of coloured tape; of the way he would slip from the worn saddle at a traffic light, straddle the cycle so unconcernedly between the shining terrors of hostile chrome and paint and stink.

To take the first step, to break the brittle spell that held her, that was the hardest part. She practised a little — as much as her small steep backyard would permit — before committing herself to the indifferent violence of the traffic, the cruel attention of the pedestrians.

On her head she wore an old riding helmet of faded brown, a survival from the days when there had been horses, paddocks and greenness in her life. She had never owned a pair of slacks so wore jodhpurs from those other days, ancient and faded but darned, pressed, neat.

The jodhpurs, oddly enough, fitted her well. She seemed younger, even, in them. Her thinned and slackened muscles and ridged sinews were concealed by the grace of the cloth's antique cut, were clothed in a kind of dignity and competence.

At least she thought so; until she mounted the rainbow machine. Then, it seemed to her, all dignity, all grace, fell away. Once she had surrendered herself to the frailty of the wheels and teetered with no equine solidity between her thin thighs she felt nothing but an echoing weakness and all the uncertainties of the strange metal.

But she rode well enough. A block or two and her waverings had vanished, the old steadiness returned. Only the fear was a constant, clenching her thin hands into pale knots on the handlebars.

Descending the last long street to the city's centre she felt deep, strange tremblings. Four, five blocks; it was a small city. She stared ahead, shortening the focus of her vision by an effort of will, ignoring the startled grins from the footpath, knowing the depths of ridicule to which she exposed herself but unable to confront it as she must her physical fear. Later, later, there would be time then: the long shamed sleepless nights when her flesh would flush and burn in the darkness.

The Dayglo flag on its orange mast gave her no confidence, nor the spinning reflectors caught in the spokes. She could rely only on her suspicion of everything that moved and held her fingers poised, strained, on the brake levers.

In the end she found that the paralysis, the anaesthesia, of her fear served her well enough. So lost was she, so caught and bound in its web, that the moving city flowed almost unregarded about her, leaving her magically untouched. The roaring buses, the belching exhausts, the clusters of traffic lights that burned palely in the hot bright day, the imperative arrows that carried her from one junction to the next — they all enveloped her so securely, so compulsively, that almost before she was aware of it she was across the bridge, pedalling sedately past the used car yards, the pawnshops, the tiny crowded supermarkets, of the unfamiliar suburb. For her, the suburb had always been a semi-mythical land of newspaper headlines and vicious uncertainties; of loudness, of drunkenness, of dull and mindless violence.

In the sudden calm of the old streets she discovered that she had forgotten to pray. And would not think of the return journey.

She made a sedate and careful turn, entered sidestreets even quieter and less crowded, cruised past oil depots, scrap merchants, obscure machinery agencies. At last she recognized in herself the small beginnings of relaxation. The echoes of unheard laughter still pursued her and in time might engulf her. But for a little she was able to contemplate again the more distant aspects of her life.

The years had struck her, of course, with her due complement of blows. But it was not, she thought, the bluntest and heaviest that were most painful. Sometimes, it seemed that the slightest and most unexpected stabs stung most, pierced deepest.

For fifteen years she and Arthur had lived — she a

spinster, he a bachelor — in houses almost opposite, almost identical; old tall houses of white weatherboard, stepped on the steel hill like rungs that climbed to the sky-line and the arterial road. The houses had been fixed, embedded in her life, and their occupants anchored as firmly to them as the houses themselves were to their own hewn basalt plinths.

She had looked forward to Arthur's retirement with the unadmitted hope that they might find some deeper sharing in the time that was left. Small things; she asked no more than those. Or admitted no more. But a habit per-haps of morning tea together, of small shopping expeditions, an extra evening a week added to their ration. So much had seemed possible once Arthur's shifts at the hospital were finished for good, his white wardsman's jacket hung up for the last time, his solid confident figure set with some degree of permanence in his own small con-fines, removed at last from the exigent wards. And she thought — he would surely find some small, new needs that she might help to meet . . .

So, as the remaining months had dwindled, her opti-mism had grown, sharpening like some happy appetite.

Then, suddenly, the emptiness had come.

It was the house. With a mere two months to go, a casual remark from Arthur. Moving. He had bought a new house across the city.

If she had ever known she had long forgotten but, of course, the house belonged to the hospital and once Arthur left the wards he must leave the house.

She canvassed all the possibilities, all the pitifully few possibilities. Perhaps she too could move? Her pride for-bade it, her finances prohibited it. A suggestion that he share her house, a lodger? Unthinkable. He valued his privacy and she suspected that he much preferred life alone. In the end, she had settled on the only possibility.

She would visit him, regularly and often; if necessary, implacably.

The idea of the bicycle had been sparked by the sight of Michael's machine. The boy, grandson of a friend of Arthur's, came each Friday evening and Saturday morning. For almost two years he had been a regular caller. It was a kindness, a small charity on Arthur's part. The boy did a few token jobs; tidied the garden, helped with cleaning, rearranged furniture unnecessarily. Arthur paid him two dollars each visit. And he came so easily, so smilingly, so casually, on his old bicycle. She had concluded reluctantly that if the boy could do it then so could she.

And so she found herself pedalling for the first time through the quiet backwaters of the unfamiliar suburb towards Arthur's new house.

She found it at last in a small cul-de-sac beside the great raw excavations of the latest outlet road. The sight of the house depressed her for a moment. It was smaller, lower, older even, than the other had been, than her own was. And somehow it seemed slightly mean and grubby. The yellow paint was peeling, the garden a thin dry jungle of weeds.

But she made allowances. It had been only a week, after all, and Arthur was handy; he would soon put it right. She dismounted and propped the bicycle against the sagging picket fence, walked in through the gate that was wedged permanently open, locked by rusted hinges. She felt suddenly hot, sweaty, disordered. Removing her helmet, she tried to bring a little quick order to her hair. She noticed then, with a small shock, that another bicycle was propped inside the gate. But it was all right, it was Michael's; she liked Michael, they liked each other. His square open face and long pale hair, his stocky wiry body, set small waves of affection in motion within the empty spaces of her life.

So she propped her own gleaming bicycle beside the

battered one, walked through the jammed gate and up the path to the front door, her sandshoes making no sound on the mossy brick paving.

The door stood open and she raised her knuckles to tap. Then heard the slight sounds of movement, of occupancy, from the living room, a pace or two from where she stood. So, instead of knocking, she stepped into the short corridor, calling as she did. They had always been on those sort of terms. It was understood.

'Hello ...'

Half blind for a moment or two from the glare outside, she saw little. The room, dim, still smelling a little musty, was very warm. Then her eyes grew accustomed to the dimness and the small tableau before her struck at her like a sudden harsh flame, searing like fire on naked skin.

On the far side of the room, under the shaded window, Arthur and the boy knelt side by side in front of the sofa. On the worn pile of the familiar beige velvet were strewn the garish covers of record albums. Arthur, on the boy's left, was reaching across to pick up a record with his left hand. His right lay lightly across the boy's shoulders, the fingers resting gently on the fabric of the thin shirt, tips just touching bare brown skin.

It seemed almost what she had seen a hundred times before — a kind of rough avuncular affection. But now, in the droop of the arm, in the touch of the fingers, she recognized — she had lacked it, longed for it often enough — the tentative and gentle sensuality of a lover's caress.

It might have been nothing; she might have glossed it over, passed it off. But at the sound of her call, at her sudden appearance in the doorway, Arthur's head had turned and his face in the dimness was twisted subtly in the contours of guilt. Its fear, its sudden animal quality, struck at her and shocked her into stillness.

No one moved except the boy, who turned and smiled a welcome.

Arthur, she knew, had seen the recognition in her face.

Under her revulsion she was sure — the boy's face told her — that it was not too late. For the boy.

'Michael,' she said, surprised at the calmness in her voice, 'come outside for a minute, there's a good boy. I want to talk to you.'

He rose obediently, smiled once at Arthur, followed her obediently out into the sunlight. The brightness seemed to her unseasonal, as if disasters belonged only to storms. At the gate she spoke to the boy.

'Michael,' she said, 'I've got bad news for you. You mustn't come back to see Arthur any more.'

He stared at her wordlessly for a moment, then opened his mouth to speak. She raised her hand sharply.

'He's sick,' she said. 'He doesn't even know it, but he's sick. And he mustn't have visitors.' She paused. How to do it? How to make certain? 'Young people particularly,' she said. 'They make loud noises, sudden movements. You'll understand, I promise, when you're older. In the meantime, remember — you mustn't come back. Will you promise?'

He nodded slowly, doubtful.

'Tell your mother what I said,' she told him. 'Exactly what I said. She'll understand. And tell her that everything is *all right*. You understand?'

'Can't I say goodbye, at least?'

She shook her head. 'It would only upset him ... please, you'd better go now, Michael ...'

The boy, head down, turned slowly away. He slid easily onto the old bicycle, rode out the gate and down the footpath at a snail's pace. At the corner he turned his head once, a final puzzled look. Then he was gone.

And she was left alone in the silent street beside the mockery of her bright machine, invaded by a loneliness so intense, a loss so enormous, that she felt suddenly weak and giddy.

Now, she thought, now is the time to pick up the bicycle, to climb on, to ride away; to shut out, to forget, to find the old familiar things ... to go back ... She wanted desperately to be gone from the mean street and the rows of low shabby houses. But she could not rid herself of the new picture that formed in her mind; Arthur, a dozen paces away, alone, the boy, his ... she made herself accept it, *think* it, *recognize* it ... his lover ... gone for ever ... and no company but his own guilt and fear.

She touched the bright bar of the bicycle, and it seemed now to be some *deux ex machina*, some mechanical saviour that would take her away from the new pain and emptiness. She clenched her fist on the sunwarmed smoothness, suddenly so friendly. Then she sighed, once, deeply, and set aside the thoughts of quiet comfort, of peace and slow untaxed decline. And she was suddenly aware that she had nursed, unknowingly through the years, a kind of brittle strength that held an imperative of its own, that she could not evade now. In the last moment, the warmth of indifferent metal against her palm, she learned the only truth that would ever be necessary: that strength was pain, that love was never a bargain, that even slight joys must be bought at the seller's price.

So she released her grip on the bicycle, stepped away, turned, and walked back up the path towards the darkness of the open doorway.

'Josef, in Transit'

Hobart. Friday
At least 100 Balt migrants will be arriving in Tasmania each
month until the end of June 1950, as the State's quota of 35,000
displaced persons coming to Australia in that period ...

Hobart *Mercury*, Saturday
26 March 1949

Josef has spent several weeks in careful examination of
the Bonegilla camp; the layout, the routine, the officials.

Finally he decides that it is time to invest a little of his
meagre capital: the dwindling supply of Lucky Strikes in
his scuffed and battered suitcase.

With this universal currency he obtains, from the local
schoolteacher who visits the camp each week, a few tubes
of oil paints, two worn-down hogshair brushes. Two
packets of Luckies.

He spends an hour with the men of the camp-
maintenance gang, and comes away with a bottle of tur-
pentine and three sheets of primed hardboard. Two more
packets of Luckies.

For several more days he observes the afternoon movements of the camp director. During this time Skulski, the
cabinetmaker, builds him a makeshift easel.

At last Josef is ready, and in the heat of the afternoon
posts himself — with paints, brushes, board, easel — at the

end of a line of huts. Quickly — he is used to working quickly — he begins to paint, sketching in the row of huts, the steel-blue of the March sky, the shifting whispers of dust, the haze-blurred horizon. Then, the picture half-done, he stops; waits, smoking nervously, fiddling at the easel, cleaning brushes, scraping at his rough palette with the broken kitchen knife. From the corner of his eye he watches the end of the path between the huts.

At last the familiar figure strides into view, turns towards Josef. The camp director.

Josef flicks at the flies about his face, leans forward, begins to paint in earnest, ignores the approaching figure. He works mechanically, apparently totally absorbed in his picture, as the director draws closer.

The trap is set. There is no way that the director can avoid, evade, him; he *must* pause, examine, admire, comment.

The director, plump and pink in neat khaki shorts, shirt and pith helmet, stops beside Josef. Teeters a little on his polished toes, edges back a little to watch over Josef's shoulder.

'Ah,' he says, his young sweating face almost invisible in the shadow of the topee's enormous brim. 'You paint, then?'

Josef starts a little, in carefully manufactured surprise. Turns, comes to respectful attention. 'Sir ... ah, yes, a little...'

'Very good, too,' says the director, cocking the great inverted bowl of his helmet judicially.

'Nothing,' says Josef, shrugging. 'A small sketch only.'

'You've studied, of course?' The director is properly impressed by the slick professionalism of the painting, by the clever tricks so despised by Josef.

'For a little,' says Josef. 'At the school of design in Budapest. Not academic ... what do you say? Commercial?'

The director nods wisely. 'And none the worse for that,

I dare say.' He notes that Josef is still standing to attention. 'Go on, go on, don't let me interrupt.'

Quickly Josef begins to splash silvered impasto high-lights on the flat images of corrugated-iron walls; specially hoarded bravura.

'Did you work at it?' asks the director. 'That is … ah, make a living?'

'Oh indeed, sir,' says Josef. Quite a good living.' He does not mention the endlessly repeated cherubs, angels, saints, madonnas, on the succession of church walls in villages whose names he has long forgotten. 'For a time …'

'Do you plan to go on with it in Australia? To teach, per-haps?'

Josef shrugs again. 'I think not … everything so new, the light so different, shapes so strange …' And here, at least, he is not counterfeiting; his cherubs, angels, saints, madonnas, seem wholly redundant in this land of bare distances and unyielding brightness. 'Besides,' he says, 'I did not complete my training.'

'Oh?' says the director.

It is time, Josef feels, for a little humour to leaven the stiffness of the interrogation. 'There was a girl,' he says, 'that I wanted to marry. I spoke to her father, but he refused his permission. "Josef," he said to me, "I like you, you are a good fellow. But my daughter will never marry an artist. Give it up, get an honest job. I don't care what it is, cart shit for all I care, but get an honest job".'

'And what did you do?' asks the director.

'I got a job,' says Josef. 'A clerk in the electricity works.'

'And got married?'

Josef smiles a little. 'She married someone else …'

'Ah …' The director, embarrassed, fidgets, prepares to move on.

It is time. Josef steps back, turns toward the director. 'I paint not only landscapes,' he says, 'but figures, portraits. Watch, sir …'

He takes a brush, picks up a little colour, and in the painted sky above the huts sketches his rehearsed version of the camp employment officer's narrow face. There is a kind of sudden magic to it, the instant conjuration of the bony face, the wing-nut ears; the blossoming of the nondescript features in the hot blue sky.

'Amazing,' says the director, stepping closer again.

'Perhaps,' says Josef a little tentatively, 'you would permit me to attempt a portrait of yourself? If you could spare an hour or so?'

The director is gratified, flattered, but doubtful. 'Well, I don't know...'

'You have a most interesting face,' says Josef boldly, staring blandly at the pink perspiring ordinariness before him. 'A challenge, to attempt the strength, the character...'

The director, of course, cannot resist.

'Halecki is to be deported,' Brodzinski tells them as they all walk slowly back to the hut from the dining hall in the cool of the evening. Halecki had found himself without papers at Naples, but had boarded the ship regardless.

'Deported!'

'No!'

'Where to?'

'How do you know?'

'It was in the papers,' says Brodzinski. 'One of the cooks told me.'

'But *deported*! Where will they send him? Not back to Poland, surely?'

Brodzinski shrugs. 'Who knows? He goes to gaol for two months, then back to Europe.'

'But surely ... not back to Poland? They wouldn't do that. Would they?'

They are all uneasy, remembering the trucks, the trains, the bayonets; cut veins, self-stranglings, blood ...

And they all fall suddenly silent.

I am painting him, thinks Josef, as I painted my cherubs: slickly, cleverly, with no more depth than the skin of paint. And he is struck, once again, by the director's resemblance — which Josef is trying very hard to evade — to a cherub; pink, round, earnest, hairless. I am as spurious, he thinks, as shallow and inconsistent as the painting. I pray no more, I laugh at priests, I reject God — yet each night I read the Bible, find myself trembling with anger at what they have done to Mindzenty, yearning for divine retribution.

Between brushstrokes the world rushes in on him, fragmented, confused, frightening. His only armour is the fragile possibility of survival, and he dares not hope too much, imposes a rigid self-ridicule at his own devious and constant cunning.

Painting the director, despising himself, he feels a strange affection for the dull young man. He is too harmless, unmenacing, ineffectual, for hate, for dislike, even for indifference.

Before Josef, seated on a hard chair, the director sways gently, sweats comfortably, stares vacantly into remembered subcontinental distances. He is an Anglo-Indian, a refugee — although he cannot think of it that way — like all the rest of them.

'You understand, sir,' says Josef, 'that it will take a little time ... a week or two, perhaps. One must work carefully, slowly, at a portrait. The subject must be learned, the character, the feeling, developed. Perhaps if we were to work for an hour or so each afternoon?'

The director nods gently, a shiny pink Buddha enshrined on a bentwood chair.

'No hurry,' he says. 'You'll be here for another week or two yet...'

As the days pass an uneasiness grows in the group. New parties arrive, old ones leave for remote destinations:

Darwin, Sydney, Newcastle, Melbourne. Soon, they know, it will be their turn.

'Where should we go?' asks Sulikowski.

'Where we are sent,' says Skulski. He feels the heat more than the others, and fears the prospect of Darwin. But he is prepared, nevertheless. 'Wherever there are jobs — they will send us, and we will go ...'

'But there is a choice,' says Kurpinski. 'You don't have to take the first job that comes along ...'

'How many times will you refuse?' asks Czarniecki. 'Don't forget those airmen. They refused once too often ...'

'What do you think, sir?' asks Sulikowski, addressing Brodzinski.

'Please don't call me "sir",' says Brodzinski. 'We must wait, Tadeusz, wait ... perhaps we will be lucky. Just wait and see.'

Josef says nothing, reads his green book, the one with the maps inside the covers.

But Josef, although he is silent, is much concerned with the matter of jobs. He does not wish to work in a city, does not fancy the prospect of two years shut in a factory making rabbit-proof fencing. He cannot comprehend the threat of the rabbits, anyway; and there are certainly more immediate and personal problems. Like most of the others, he does not wish to work in the hot places; and he would prefer, at least for a time, to remain with his fellow Europeans. But — and there lies the difficulty — while there is a certain amount of choice, that choice is limited, and governed by many unknown factors. No one, not even the employment officer, is able to spell out the ground rules with any precision. Much seems to depend upon the number and source of the labour requisitions which arrive at the camp office. At the moment they are recruiting for a cement factory, and this does not appeal at all to Josef.

He needs a little time to consider, and must pace his portrait accordingly.

'Who,' asks Skulski, 'is this Sharkey? This one they say they will arrest?'

They have eaten their stew, beans and potatoes, their treacle pudding and custard. The food is distending their bellies, but not yet reaching their muscles; their limbs are still much too thin, mismatched appendages linked oddly to plump trunks.

'Sharkey?' says Brodzinski. 'I don't know. Bruno?'

Bruno can read the newspapers. He sits now, elbows on the table, smoking quietly, focused on distances that lie wholly within him. He stirs, sighs a little. 'He's a communist,' he says. 'He has been saying things about the Russians ...'

'What things?'

'That if Russian troops landed in Australia, then Australian workers would welcome them ...'

'What? No, it can't be ...'

'True,' says Bruno.

'It wouldn't happen, it couldn't ...'

'But who is he?'

Bruno shrugs. 'A unionist, a leader.'

They are all confused. Sulikowski frowns, his round face creased in puzzlement. Skulski glowers. Czarniecki shakes his head slowly. 'It's not possible, it couldn't be ...'

'Anyway,' says Josef, 'don't worry, they'll put him in gaol.'

'They ought to shoot the bastard,' says Skulski. 'Better, send him here, let *us* shoot him ...'

'But *would* the Australians welcome the Russians?' asks Sulikowski.

'Don't be stupid,' says Czarniecki. '*No one* welcomes the Russians ...'

The director breaks the silence, but not his pose.

'I think,' he says, 'that I will go to Queensland. Eventually. The climate, you know. I'm used to the heat. And it gets very cold here in winter, very cold.' He caresses the beads of sweat from his short upper lip, flicks a quick glance at Josef, apprehensive in case his small movement has been noticed. 'India,' he goes on, 'the heat ... I'm used to it. And the natives. I believe there are natives in Queensland. Perhaps a job in the administration ...'

The silence settles again as Josef continues to stroke safely at the board with a dry brush. He tries to think of a way to broach the problem of his own destination.

Unexpectedly, the director solves the problem for him.

'What about you, Josef?' he asks, eyes fixed firmly on the faded picture of the King that hangs between a set of dull brass gongs. 'Where do you fancy?'

'Ah,' says Josef, assuming an appropriate humility, 'I will, of course, go where I am sent. A matter of luck. Who can tell? Unlike you, sir, I find that the heat distresses me. Still ...'

'I think,' says the director, 'that Tasmania might suit you, Josef. The climate, I believe, is not dissimilar to that of Europe.'

Josef nods slowly. He has already reached the same conclusion. But the cement factory is in Tasmania.

'And of course there are no flies there,' says the director.

'No flies?' says Josef, surprised.

'So I am led to believe,' says the director.

'One would prefer,' says Josef humbly, worrying a blob of chrome green, 'to avoid factories if at all possible.'

'We have a requisition,' says the director, 'from the Hydro-Electric Commission in Tasmania. Fifty men. It might suit. In the bush of course,' and he flicks another quick glance at Josef, 'for the full two years.'

Josef nods cautiously.

'On the other hand,' says the director, 'we expect to hear

from the Postmaster-General's Department within a week or so … that might be even better.'

'Oh?' says Josef.

'It would still be in the bush,' says the director. 'But the Hydro-Electric job, I believe, involves the digging of quite large holes … sixteen or twenty feet square. The Postmaster's holes, on the other hand, are relatively small … a matter of three feet by two …'

Josef makes his decision quickly. The portrait, a little over-pink due to his limited palette, but augmented with a flush of spurious distinction, is almost finished. Deftly, Josef smudges the lower portion of the face. Stands back, purses his lips.

'How is it going?' asks the director.

'There is a little problem,' says Josef, 'with the line of the jaw — the firmness, the strength, it is not easy to achieve without a degree of subtlety … patience, patience is needed.'

'How much longer?' asks the director.

'Another week,' says Josef. 'Perhaps a little more …'

The director is silent for a moment.

'Josef,' he says at last, 'if you should hear your name called by the employment office, just keep out of the way for a few days … in a camp this size you will have no trouble, I am sure …'

Josef, too, is sure. He is an expert at keeping out of the way in camps.

He begins afresh on the jawline, working very slowly and carefully.

'Would we have to join a union?' asks Czarniecki.

They are seated, the seven of them, on two beds; a double line of earnest faces bent over clasped hands and cigarettes. They talk quietly, clustered in isolation from the other men scattered through the hut in random evening pastimes.

'I don't think so,' says Josef. 'It is a government job, you see. Surely they can have no unions in the government.'

'Should we ask?' says Kurpinski.

Josef shakes his head. 'The less we ask the better. We just go along to the office and sign our names when the time comes.'

'And the work? Just digging holes?'

Josef shrugs. 'I don't know. That's all he said. Digging holes, in the bush.'

'What for? What are the holes for?'

'For poles, I suppose. You know, telephone wires.'

'Whereabouts? Where would we go?' asks Sulikowski.

Josef is beginning to grow short-tempered. '*I* don't know ... how should *I* know! In Tasmania, in the bush, digging holes ... where we are sent, where else ...'

'Rautner and Goldstein and that lot are going to Melbourne,' says Czarniecki. 'They say there is good business there ...'

'They are Jews,' says Kurpinski. 'They go always where there is good business.'

'You want to go to Melbourne?' says Sulikowski to Czarniecki. 'You want to work in a pickle factory for two years? Go on then, pickle your dick ...'

Silence falls over the group.

At length Sulikowski speaks to Brodzinski, who has said nothing. 'What do *you* think, Doctor? What should we do?'

'Don't call me "Doctor",' says Brodzinski absently. He is quiet for a moment or two. 'First of all,' he says at last, 'we must decide if we want to stay together. If we do, then we must all agree ...'

No one speaks. During the weeks in the camp they have come to think of their small group as something natural, complete, permanent, a small unity in the confusion of their new world. It has never occurred to them that it might be broken up. Josef is suddenly very conscious, once more, that he is a lone Hungarian among the Poles. There is Bruno, of course, but somehow he doesn't seem to count.

'Well,' asks Brodzinski, looking from face to face, 'do we stay together?'

One by one they nod. It is something, an affirmation of some kind, some protection against the unknown. They have created their tribe.

'Very good,' says Brodzinski. 'Josef — how many men will this … P.G.M.? … need?'

'P.M.G.,' says Josef. 'I think, from what the director says, about a dozen. Perhaps a dozen and a half.'

'Then,' says Brodzinski, 'we must decide now if it is what we all wish. We know nothing of these jobs. But it seems that we have a good chance of staying together if we take them. And it can't be that bad, out in the forest. The climate, too, like Europe, Josef says …'

'Not me,' says Josef. 'That is what the director says. But the book says that there is snow in winter, in the mountains.'

'Well,' says Brodzinski, 'we must guess, take a chance.' He looks once more at the faces about him, speaks to them one by one.

'Josef?'

'Yes, of course.'

'Stanislas?'

Skulski shrugs. 'Why not?'

'Janek?'

Kurpinski grins his sly dark grin. 'Yes, why not? Maybe I'll get a desk job — someone will have to count all those holes!'

'Tadeusz?'

'Yes.' Sulikowski's broad face is serious, his forehead crinkled. 'I think it's good that we will be away from people for a while…'

For a moment there is silence. They have all been part of too many crowds. But Sulikowski's crowds are mostly ghosts. His first camp was Auschwitz.

'Stefan?'

'As long as there's food,' says Czarniecki, 'and they leave us alone.'

'Bruno?' Brodzinski's voice softens a little as he looks at Veske's face. He has said nothing, his calm, lined, almost handsome face the only one stamped with a certain apartness. He is an outsider, in a way that even Josef can never be. Now he smiles, gently.

'I'd like to go with you, Mr Brodzinski,' he says, and looks down at the floor, waiting, as if for a verdict.

'Good,' says Brodzinski. 'Then we all go. To dig holes...'

Josef returns to the hut in the late afternoon with palette, brushes, easel; no picture. He puts the bundle down quickly on his bed, hurries across to Brodzinski, who is dozing, lays a hand on his shoulder.

'The requisition has arrived,' he says. 'They want fourteen men ... we must go to the employment office first thing tomorrow.'

Brodzinski sits up, blinking. 'Yes, yes ... but ... only fourteen! What if others are there before us? If they sign first?'

Josef is already back at this own bed, rummaging in his suitcase. Out comes the last carton of Lucky Strikes. '*We* will be first, we must be — I am going now to see the employment officer ...'

And he has gone, clutching his last negotiable assets.

'Who else is going with us? asks Kurpinski.

They are busy packing their meagre belongings, although it will be another day before they leave. There is tension in them, now, a sense of uncertainties, of new possibilities suddenly opening before them; and an uneasiness at the prospect of leaving the bland routine of the camp, the last real crowds of a transported Europe.

'Some Latvians … Liepaja, I think, Urch … and four Yugoslavs, Bavic, Hristic, that lot …'

'Will they be with us?' asks Czarniecki. 'On the same job?'

'Holy Christ,' says Josef, 'I don't know … how can I know?' He finds that his hands are trembling a little, with some kind of unfocused apprehension.

'Be calm,' says Brodzinski. 'We will know soon enough. It will be only a few days more.'

'Where will we be going?' asks Skulski. 'The mountains?'

'Maybe,' says Josef.

'The mountains,' says Sulikowski. 'That would be good!' His eyes are wide with excitement, like a child at the beginning of a long-awaited holiday. Josef finds suddenly that he envies Sulikowski his enthusiasm, and is suddenly sad.

'Wait and see,' says Brodzinski, 'wait and see.'

Josef takes out the green book with the maps, and they all begin to wait.

On the train Josef watches the land, still wide, bare, intimidating, slip by once again. This time there are no food-laden tables at way stations, no speeches, no pink-cheeked matrons, no steaming urns. Now they are only fourteen, a fragment barely discernable, already partly submerged in the silences of the new land. Little by little the great tide of which they were part is disappearing, thinning into smaller and smaller streams, reaching for new and distant destinations. Soon there would be no group, no common identity at all; only single individuals, isolated, finally alone.

Watching Bruno, who alone among them seems content, self-contained, unexpectant in the shifting world, Josef feels within him sudden desperate and feverish uncertainties; and is afraid, knowing that in the future that is no longer distant, evanescent, he must face some moment of decision, of final acceptance; a moment which will determine whether survival is still possible.

Wait, he thinks. Wait. For a pessimist there are always possibilities. Shelter, food, holes to dig. Twelve pounds a fortnight. Two years to learn something, to find something.

At least, he thinks, they have not been prodigal with their promises ...

Uphill Runner

Old Uncle Bennet, who was nobody's uncle that I know of, woke me just before dawn and I stumbled out of my sleeping bag in the corner of the farmhouse kitchen. There was a pulsing orange glow from the grate of the old range against the back wall. The window was a square of cold pearly metal that seemed to suck the warmth from the room. Uncle, stooped and dirty as he had been last year, and the year before that, and as far back, almost, as I could remember, lifted the steaming kettle from the stove and filled a dented enamel teapot. Waiting for it to draw, I went and stood beside him at the stove, holding my hands over the hot iron plates. I shivered. There was no sound from beyond the door where the other three still slept in the only beds. It was the first year that there had been only four of us. I had always shared the kitchen with Gerry.

I went to the corner and pulled on my clothes over my longjohns, slipped on my boots, and then took the cup of steaming tea that Uncle Bennet gave me. I walked out onto the long verandah.

Across the river, I could see the dim outline of the hill, dark and flat, not yet touched by the sun. In the river hollows the ti-trees were still hidden by the valley fog that lay like dirty cotton-wool at the foot of the long slope. The lumpy pasture that reached up to the house was studded with the dim shapes of tussocks. In the half-light small clumps of bracken looked like crouching animals. I took a sip of the hot tea, set the cup down on the bench by the door, and lit a cigarette. Despite the cold, it was the best part of the morning, when the sky is clear and soft, and the big silver wattles are so heavy with dew that they look frosted, that time when the light strengthens as you watch. You can fix your eyes on a shape fifty paces away, and you can't tell whether it's a tussock, or a stump, or what it is, and you fix the shape in your mind and look away, and you look back in a minute or two and the shape is clear and sharp in every detail. And you sight another shape, just a little further away, and you do it again. And soon, almost before you know it, you've got shooting light.

And I thought: no rabbits for Gerry today. And I wondered again what had kept him away this year.

When the light was clear to the river, and the tea was gone, I went back into the dim kitchen. Uncle was frying sausages in a big black pan. As I came in he started to break eggs into the hot fat, and the room was filled suddenly with the sizzling belly-clutching smells.

'Better git 'em out,' said Uncle. And I moved towards the bedroom door. But before I got there it swung open and Vinny stumbled, blinking, into the kitchen. He was wearing his long underwear, and he had a dirty grey blanket wrapped round his shoulders. His short straw-coloured hair was tousled, sticking up at all angles. He yawned, but his blue eyes were as sharp and clear as ever. He went over to the stove and kissed Uncle Bennet on the stubbly cheek.

'Good old boy,' he said, and dropped his blanket about his feet. He picked up the toasting-fork and speared a smoking sausage.

Old Uncle chuckled a little, spooning fat over the eggs. 'You got pretty drunk last night,' he said.

'Drunk and broke,' said Vinny, juggling the hot sausage. 'That bloody Con, he's got trained cards.'

'You get drunk, you shouldn't play cards,' said Uncle Bennet.

'By God,' said Vinny, suddenly dead still, 'you're right, Uncle! If only I'd thought of that.' He turned and winked at me. Then, his mouth full of soft mashed meat, 'He hasn't come yet?'

I shook my head, started to put plates out on the rickety table.

'Shit.' He was suddenly deflated.

'Never mind,' I said. 'He might come yet.' But I didn't really believe it.

Vinny speared another sausage disconsolately.

Uncle began to fill plates. He looked up at me. 'Better git them other two out, else there'll be no sausages left ...'

So I went to call them.

We ate our breakfast quickly, standing round the table. I began to feel a little queasy, because I'd drunk too much whisky the night before. But I chewed on, forcing the food down, knowing that I'd feel better for it. Blue was silent, looking sleepy and sardonic as he chewed. Con looked pale and ill, but he'd looked pale and ill in the mornings for as long as I could remember. He looked at me once, raised his eyebrows. I shook my head, and he shrugged. Uncle poured more tea, and we drank it slowly, standing round the stove.

And I had a moment, then, of seeing us the way an outsider might; four soft-skinned middle-aged townsmen in old clothes, eating bad food and drinking bitter tea as if we liked it, at a time of day that we saw maybe once a year. And waiting to go through a ritual a generation old, and strangely unsettled because there were only four of us, and not five, and feeling childishly that because of it the luck might somehow be broken, that this year the old magic might not work.

But then the tea was finished, and it was full daylight. And it was time for the rabbits, and Gerry wasn't coming this year. So in the end the four of us trooped silently out onto the verandah.

No one seemed to want to make a start. Vinny sat in the sagging old wicker chair fiddling with his bootlace, and Con spent a long time counting bullets. Blue stood idly working the bolt of the old .22 single-shot that he's owned for more than thirty years. We all had those old single-shots. It was part of the ritual. The afternoon would be different, but for the morning it was just the old rifles.

'Come on,' I said, 'for Christ's sake ...' The sun was edging up over the hills to the east.

And, reluctantly, they followed me down the steps.

Vinny heard it first, then the rest of us, and we stopped there, grouped at the bottom of the steps, our ears cocked, like a bunch of nervous schoolgirls.

The distant whine of the car's engine grew louder.

'It's him!' said Vinny.

No one said anything.

'It *is*,' said Vinny.

Still we waited.

And then the car, Gerry's bright red Alfa, swung in from the road and surged up the white curl of gravel road half a mile away. Suddenly we were all laughing and slapping each other on the back.

'I told you!' said Vinny. 'I told you he'd come!'

The others all looked sheepish, and pleased, and I suppose that I did too. Because, when you came down to it, I was closer to Gerry than any of the others.

The Alfa slewed to a halt ten yards from the steps, scattering gravel on our boots. We could see Gerry behind the wheel. He switched off the engine and just sat there for a minute. The small metallic noises of the cooling engine sounded loud in the chill air. Then he opened the door and got out.

I saw that he still had a suit on, a little creased and

wrinkled, and a tie dragged down from his open collar. And as the first of the sun took his square Irish face, I could see that his eyes were a little bloodshot, and that he hadn't shaved.

'Came straight from a party,' he said, looking at us almost hesitantly, yet with a trace of that same old familiar boyishness. 'Bet you thought I wasn't coming, eh?'

'You can't go shooting like that,' said Blue, nodding at the suit.

'Why not?' said Gerry, and smiled a little. He looked at me then, and I could see that he was very tired. 'I'll just borrow a pair of Uncle's gumboots.' And he was gone, running easily up the old steps, as if he wasn't really fifty years old at all, as if nothing could ever stop him.

And we all stood there looking after him, smiling like idiots as the day grew brighter around us.

Gerry walked beside me on the way down to the flat, slopping a little in his borrowed boots.

'Hard night?' I said.

'Are there any easy ones?' He turned a little to look at me, and for a moment I seemed to see strange shadows in his grey eyes. But then he laughed softly, looked down to check his rifle, and I thought that I must have imagined it.

It had all begun before we were even out of high school. Five wild kids who found an old farmer who, for a few quid, would feed us for a weekend, let us shoot his rabbits and hares, who didn't care if we swore and drank whisky and played poker all night and spewed on his doorstep. It lasted only a couple of years, then. Because for Gerry and me there was Korea, for the others university. But afterwards, when we were all back in the old town again, someone — I think it was Vinny — talked us into starting again. And for some reason we did. And soon we were thirty, and then forty. And still we came, once a year, to the rundown farm, for two days of whisky and poker and shooting. And the strange thing is that we all still enjoyed it; I know that I looked forward to it for months, arranged my timetable, almost my life, around it. I don't know why it should have taken such a hold on us, but it had. And it never made any difference that we didn't see much of each other for the rest of the year. For that one weekend all the barriers dropped, and we were back in that faraway never-never land where it had all started.

The afternoon would be serious, but the morning was for fun. It had always been that way. We spread out in a line across the flat, and walked westward towards the place where the bush came down to the river a couple of miles away. The ground was covered with thin grass and sags and clumps of bracken. Everything was still wet with dew. We started the first rabbit within a minute or two, and Con loosed off a shot. But it was gone before he had sighted properly. His shot raised another pair, though, and Blue got one of them.

By the time we had gone half a mile everyone had taken at least one shot, except Gerry. He had never even lifted his rifle.

'What's wrong?' I asked him while we waited for Blue to pick up another rabbit from the river bank.

'Nothing,' he said. 'Hangover, that's all.'

And, as if to prove it, he took the next rabbit with a headshot at forty yards. He was always the best of us, Gerry. But I was beside him when he bent over to pick up the carcase, and in the sudden dimness under the black-wood tree his face was flooded with a sudden unmistakable sadness, a desolation that startled me.

'For Christ's sake,' I said, 'what is it? What's the matter?'

But he just shook his head. 'Nothing, mate,' he said. 'Just old age creeping on.'

But I couldn't help worrying. Because to tell the truth he'd been a little ... different ... over the past year. He still smiled and joked, and he was still a lot of fun, a good mate. But there was a kind of *edge* to him, not quite strain, but something like it. His practice was all right as far as I knew, and he'd left the dull parts, like conveyancing, behind years before, and was into the exciting stuff, putting deals together, making things happen. He was even into some of the big developments, and if they hadn't turned out as well as they might have, he was solid enough. And his wife, well, we'd all known Jenny for as long as we'd known him, and there wasn't much to go wrong there.

'How long is it?' he said suddenly, coming to an abrupt halt. 'Since we started coming here?'

'Too long,' I said. 'Too many years.'

'No,' he said, and there was that awful sadness, almost like a longing in his voice, 'not long enough ...'

But by then we had run all the rabbits and it was time to turn back. And all the way to the farmhouse he was silent, swinging the dead rabbit in one hand, cradling the old rifle under his arm, and not smiling at all.

It wasn't that he had ever smiled a lot. It was just that his face had a kind of smiling *cast* to it. And nothing ever seemed to scare him. He was probably the calmest, the least *afraid* person that I've ever known. I'd always known that, right from the time we were kids together. But I never quite realized just how deep it went until Korea. One place, one time, one event is stamped indelibly on my memory.

It was in the bad days, some of the worst, our unit pinched in a narrow bottleneck, the pressure constant, our lives a round of dull misery, snow melting then freezing again to gelid mud, cold that day after day settled deeper in our bones; periods of savage shelling, interspersed with hours of awful quiet, broken only by the bitter whipcracks of sniper fire and the dull thudding of grenades that arced in from the launchers across the river.

Our dugout was like an oversized grave, half-roofed with rotten canvas and ankle-deep in mud. There were three of us in it that night; Gerry — who was captain by then — me, and a platoon runner. Gerry was busy on the radio to HQ, and I was talking to the runner. We all heard the thump, the tearing of the perished canvas, saw the ugly shape of the grenade that dropped onto the table, bounced to the floor between us. The runner and I both threw ourselves over backward onto the ground. I remember lying there, my face in the mud, counting. I got up to four before I realized that Gerry's voice hadn't stopped. He was still talking on the radio, just as calm as ever, as if the grenade simply didn't exist. When I'd counted to ten I got up. I knew by then that the grenade was a dud. And Gerry was still sitting there, talking, and he smiled at me as if it was all a great joke.

Some of them, if they got that way, began to do crazy things, take insane risks. But not Gerry. He never changed at all. It was just that he never seemed to be afraid.

In the afternoon it was time for the hares, and for the serious shooting. The mood began to change, as it always did, over Uncle Bennet's terrible lunch. As we chewed on the stringy steak and scooped up the watery potatoes, we seemed to withdraw into ourselves a bit, even Vinny.

We all took out our guns, mostly expensive autos or pumps. Only Gerry had a hammer gun, an old and beautiful Greener double that had been his father's. We sat there on the verandah sorting out cartridges, giving the guns a last rub, looking up now and then at the long hill over the creek. The weather was no longer blue, but grey, and a light chill wind blew down the valley. I shivered a little, decided to put on a pullover under my shooting jacket.

Gerry had borrowed bits and pieces from all of us, and he must have been warm enough, but he looked strangely pinched, all the same.

We set off down the track to the bridge, not talking much. At the bottom of the hill we climbed through the last wire fence at the edge of the paddock. The land sloped up now, open bush and neglected pasture all the way up to the top of the hill. It was the place for the hares, and we spread out, twenty paces apart, and began the slow ascent.

Before we had been moving for more than a couple of minutes Con flushed the first hare. It streaked up the hill, long and lean and grey, moving faster than seemed possible.

Con missed with his first shot, but caught it with the next, just at the limit of range. We moved forward again slowly, Con frowning to himself over the missed shot.

Vinny took the next one, picking it up almost before it had got well started, blowing it head over heels into the ferns. We waited while he went to pick it up.

'Ever wondered,' said Gerry suddenly, 'why they always run uphill?' He had moved over until he was only a few yards from me.

I thought for a moment, shook my head.

'They always do, don't they?'

'Yes, they do.'

'They'd go faster on the flat,' he said, 'or downhill, wouldn't they?'

'I guess so.'

'Rabbits run mostly downhill, don't they?'

I thought for a moment. 'I suppose they do.'

'Then why do hares run uphill?'

'I don't know,' I said. He was looking up towards the top of the hill.

'I think,' he said, 'that they do it because they can run uphill faster than anything *else* can ...'

I didn't say anything. And the line moved forward again, so Gerry went back to his place.

We came back halfway through the afternoon. The day was very grey now, and cold, and the wind was fluffing the silver wattles and rattling the bracken. There were eleven hares when we laid them out by the steps. Con had shot five, Vinny three, Blue two. I had taken only one, and felt somehow uncomfortable about that, even. Because Gerry, the best shot among us, had not even fired his gun. He looked a little down, but then so did we all for some reason. And it wasn't that it was all over for another year. It was something more, and it had to do with Gerry.

This year there was no waiting around for a last drink, a final yarn. Everyone seemed eager to get away, almost indecently eager, and a little ashamed of their eagerness. Oddly, it was Vinny who was the first to go, mumbling about the weather, dropping his gear into the boot of his car anyhow, laughing half-heartedly, and not meeting anyone's eyes as he climbed behind the wheel. Then it was Con, and then Blue. Old Uncle had gone to drive his cows in for milking, and only Gerry and I were left.

He sighed, looking very tired now, his face flushed and windburned, his eyes still a little bloodshot. 'I think,' he said, 'I'll go back up the hill, see if I can get a hare to take home.' He smiled, his eyes crinkling a little. 'I can't go home without one, can I?'

'Take mine,' I said.

He smiled again, but it seemed to take him a great effort. 'I couldn't do that, could I?'

'No,' I said, 'I suppose not.'

'I'll just go back for half an hour or so,' he said, picking up his gun. 'Don't wait for me, old buddy, I'll see you soon, anyway.'

'All right,' I said.

And he was gone, striding quickly away down the paddock, the wind stirring his hair, tugging at the skirts of his jacket. He didn't look back.

I felt very dull and heavy and stupid as I gathered up my gear and stowed it in the car.

I started the car, took one last look at Gerry's figure in the distance, and drove off. But I didn't drive far. Round the first bend, where the high hedge of blackberries hid the house and the hill, I stopped. I just sat there for the time it took to smoke a cigarette. Then I got out and walked back to the gate and leaned on it, looking towards the house. The only sound was the wind in the big gum tree beside me. A thin drift of smoke straggled from the chimney of the house, grey smoke from a grey house, and Gerry's car was a blood-bright splash in the yard.

Something was wrong. I didn't know what, or how, or why. But I knew.

And then I heard the thin distant sound of the shot. It came from the direction of the hill, half a mile away.

I started running. I don't know why I ran. After all, he'd said that he was going after hares. But I ran, all the same, and I kept on running; past the house, past the red car, over the bridge, along the flat towards the bottom of the hill.

I found him there, at the fence. I stopped twenty yards away. I didn't want to go any closer. But I knew that I had to, so in the end I did.

I remember thinking, while I stood there looking down at him, my breath rasping, my chest pumping, what a good job he'd made of it. Everything just right. I'd never known him to climb a fence without breaking his gun, but I could see from the way it was lying that he'd pushed it through the strands of wire holding it by the barrel. One of the hammers had caught, and he'd given it a jerk to free it. The hammer had been pulled back almost far enough to cock it, and then slipped free and fallen. He'd been holding the end of the barrel close to his chest, and that was that. And it was all just right, and I made certain that I didn't touch a thing.

So there was nothing to do, not there on that bloody lonely grey hill, under that cold empty sky, and I turned away and left him, and walked slowly back to the house. I wasn't really crying, but I felt as if I was.

I found Uncle Bennet in the cowshed and sent him off to phone the police from the farm down the road. He just shook his head when I told him, didn't say anything.

When he had gone I went and sat on the steps and lit a cigarette. I didn't want to look at the hill. In fact I didn't want to look at anything. After a while I stubbed out the cigarette and walked over to his car. The envelope with my name on it was lying on the seat. I suppose he knew that I wouldn't really leave like that.

I tore the envelope open and took out the single sheet of paper. It was neatly typed, just his name signed, so I knew that he'd written it before he'd even come out to the farm.

'Sorry, old mate,' it said, 'but I got caught in the last zoning squeeze. I've been tickling the peter, and I'm into my trust funds for about sixty thousand. Do the best you can for Jenny and the kids. Love, Gerry.'

I went back to the steps and sat down. It seemed so bloody stupid, so bloody useless. I didn't have that kind of money myself, but it would have taken maybe two phone calls to get him covered. If he'd only told me. If he'd only been able to tell me. And I thought again of Korea, and about how he had never seemed afraid of anything. And for some reason I thought about what he'd said about the hares running uphill. And then I didn't want to think about anything at all for a while, so I took out my lighter and set fire to the letter. I held it until it was almost gone, and then I let the wind take the last charred fragment and whirl it away into nothing. And then I just sat on the steps smoking and waiting and watching the grey clouds that were getting darker and heavier and racing faster and faster across the sky.

Room-mate

My first landlady.

Mrs Peach, a woman (a lady, she would have said) of strict propriety and awesome bulk; of tight-drawn dark hair and incipient moustaches; of breast-bulged floral dresses and run-down slippers; widowed, daughtered, almost son-in-lawed. Grace, her skinny, sallow, nineteen-year-old only child was engaged to a skinny, sallow ex-sailor, Ralph. Their courting — at least that part of it perpetrated in public — was placid, domestic, dull. They were dull people, all of them, peopling a dull house, a dim house, a house filled with the smells of wax polish, over-boiled cabbage and strong yellow soap.

My first lodgings.

A cramped tall fifty-year-old house huddled against the high blank wall of the football ground; weatherboard and roughcast, brick Mayan verandah posts; high ceilings, runnered hall, varnished boards, dimness, dimness everywhere. Bathroom and lavatory tacked on at the back, skillion-roofed, an afterthought of a generation cleaner — or dirtier — then the one that had built the house. Small shadowed brick-paved backyard and a weedy lane where I parked my motor bike.

My first room-mate.

Mr Ryan. Old, I thought then, in his middle fifties at least. Always well dressed, neat dark suit, clean shirt, quiet tie, grey felt hat, bright black shoes. And blind. Each morning he would step out with his white stick and tap confidently along the quiet streets to the blind workshop two left-hand right-angles of the footpath away. And in the evenings return. Sometimes I would be there, in our room, when he came in. He would speak to me — his voice was low, pleasant — and take off his hat. And immediately he would look very different. Baldness had eroded his greying brown hair, and the top of his head was pale and smooth. Without the shelter of his hat-brim his face was tired and puffy, the skin coarse and covered with a speckling of bluish pits. The blank opacity of his glasses, with their black side-pieces, took on a cruel and clownish aspect. He seemed suddenly naked, exposed.

He had been blind, he told me, since he was seventeen. One day, in the mine where he worked, he had been tamping charges when one had exploded in his face.

I was a little nervous of him in the beginning. But that soon passed. I can see now that he went out of his way to ease the small strand of tension; he would ask me to choose a tie for him to match his socks; to locate his matches; to read a football programme for him. Small things, but soon my nervousness faded.

Our room was large, a bed on each side, two wardrobes, two dressing tables, two chairs, two small bedside tables. A window between the beds, with a view of the lane, a blank brick wall, and my motor bike. Gravy-coloured linoleum, a large greyish-pink carpet square, one overhead light, one bedlamp. Mr Ryan never knew of course when the lights were on, and sometimes would pause uncertainly when he came in, waiting for some small sound to notify my presence. Often I found myself signalling with some slight and unnecessary movement.

He slept badly, and often he would play his portable radio — with an earphone — late into the night. I would hear, sometimes, the ghost of a faint tinny whisper. Sometimes too, dozing or waking from sleep in the darkness,

I would hear strange shakings from his bed, regular rhythmical shakings. I thought that he was masturbating, and felt a kind of shamed pity for him, beyond the pity at his blindness. But one night I dozed off with the light on and woke later to the shakings and bed-squeakings from his side of the room. I opened my eyes. He was sitting up in bed, the blankets thrown back, rubbing and massaging his feet, his toes, between his toes, with a towel. I don't know why, tinea, something like that perhaps. The light from my bedlamp struck at him, touching his fleshy face, his full pale lips, the pit-marks with their kernels of forty-year-old coal dust, the naked red cavities of his empty eye sockets, with a ruthless chiaroscuro. He sat there, rubbing, rocking, the bed springs squeaking, a trickle of moisture on his cheek. I lay still, aware somehow that to move, to switch out the light, to reveal my waking presence, would be intolerable. In the end, after the rubbing had stopped and he had lain back, I went to sleep with the light still burning.

On one other night I saw him towelling furiously at his empty eye sockets, as if to quell some fearful itch.

We ate our meals in the dining room, directly across the hall from our bedroom, a room filled with cheap dark furniture, dustless, oiled and shining; grey stags reared in grey mist on the comfortless walls, and the air was brittle with unvoiced constraints. The food, generous quantities of plain mean food, was served by Mrs Peach, along with platitudes, dead as plastic flowers, that issued in a carefully rationed stream from her small pursed mouth. When her haunches had vanished, swaying, through the kitchen door we would fall again into tentative cautious conversation with our fellow boarder.

Miss Archer was a spinster — perhaps thirty-six, thirty-seven — neat, sharp-chinned, quick, with dark wavy hair and eyes like black olives. She was a clerk in the office of a city solicitor, and there clung to her an air of sly legal caution. She was permanently ambiguous. I felt sometimes that she was laughing at us behind her mask of composure and silent omniscience. She was a little acid, her humour soured. Sometimes, attracted in spite of myself by her neat frame and scrubbed femininity, I was tempted — in my nineteen-year-old arrogance — to try my luck with her. But always, intimidated by her vinegary condescension, I held back. Still, sometimes at night, groping myself in my warm bed, I would think of her alone in the room just along the hall.

But at mealtimes my fantasies would fade, dispelled by the realities of her actual presence; her straight back, her disciplined fingers, her quick knowing looks. I fancied even, from the quiet mockery of her glances, that she was aware of my nocturnal lusts.

Mr Ryan ate his food with economical and precise movements of knife, fork and spoon. The sensitivity of his fingers seemed transmitted to the cutlery, and he located the food on his plate with uncanny accuracy. Blobs and strings escaped only occasionally to his chin or lap. And it was impossible, of course, for either Miss Archer or me to call them to his notice. Even her self-possession was unequal to that.

While Miss Archer's life, outside office hours, seemed to revolve around a weekly visit to the cinema and an occasional meal with a friend (female), Mr Ryan had a number of interests; the workshop where they made door-mats, baskets, brushes; music; radio serials; and, above all, football. He was a committee member of the local club, and arranged dances and social evenings, attended training sessions, committee meetings, drank with members and players at the local pub. And within these limits he seemed content, and went through the days with a kind of unsad resignation. He seldom spoke of his blindness, and then only lightly.

Although mealtimes were never actively unpleasant, they were dull and constrained, and I was always glad to escape at their end. Usually in the evenings it was to my bed and a book. I earned £7/10/-, board cost me £5, and there was never much left over for social life. So I spent a lot of time that winter in our room. It was not unpleasant, the electric radiator warming the room, Mr Ryan's radio playing softly, a book, a cup of cocoa and a biscuit before sleep.

He was really a pleasant and considerate room-mate, Mr Ryan, once we got used to each other. And he was discreet. On more than one occasion I was hauled home drunk by my friends, in through the front door, down the dark hallway, and dumped on my bed. He never mentioned those occasions, simply ignored them.

So did Mrs Peach for that matter, although her mouth would be pursed a little tighter next day; I could not doubt that she had heard the sound of my heels dragging on the runner as I was borne past her bedroom door.

In that household boarders certainly weren't treated as members of the family; Mrs Peach maintained a distanced formality. But neither were they treated as transients. Mr Ryan had been there for seven years, Miss Archer for five. It was never plainly stated, but the house was, if not our home, at least our *residence.* And Mr Ryan, even more than Miss Archer, seemed firmly and permanently entrenched.

So when he left we all felt a tremor, a thrill of shock, as if the earth had shifted slightly beneath our feet; we felt that sting of reluctant belief that touches us when some sudden change leaves each of us potentially naked, unprotected before the world.

It was a Sunday afternoon. I had left the bike at home and taken the bus to the museum. When I got back Mrs Peach met me at the front door. She must have been waiting, watching from behind the white gauze of her bay-windowed eyrie above the bare and narrow garden.

— There's something I have to tell you, she said. Mr Ryan is leaving.

I can't remember whether I spoke, or just gaped.

— It's very unpleasant, she went on.

I couldn't imagine what was coming.

— I was standing at the side gate, she said, talking to Mrs Gargan from next door. I looked down the lane, and there was Mr Ryan at the window … he was … exposing himself … relieving himself out the window… I had to ask him to leave, of course … he's going tonight …

I went down the hall and into our room not knowing quite what to expect, what to say. Mr Ryan, neatly dressed as always, had his back to me packing his suitcase on the bed. He heard me come in, and after a moment he turned round.

— Did Mrs Peach tell you what happened? he asked.

— No, I said, she just told me you were leaving.

He spoke, said something, I can't remember what. Perhaps he told me what had happened, why he did it, I don't know. Later it seemed to me that he must have thought that it was already dark outside, and no one would see. But at the time I was confused, filled with a deafening turmoil of embarrassment, pity, shame, even disgust. And all the time there was an almost overpowering urge to giggle. In my mind was the picture of him dangling his dong out the window in front of those two old gawping biddies.

Within ten minutes he was gone. It was the last time I saw him, and his name was never mentioned in the house again. Once the gate had clicked behind him I went out into the lane to see if he had peed on my motor bike. But it was out of the line of fire, and dry.

My first conspiracy.

At tea Miss Archer and I sat opposite each other, almost wordless. Our sparse conversation was fabricated laboriously to avoid any mention of Mr Ryan. I was conscious of testing each sentence in my mind before offering it; and I suspect that Miss Archer did the same. We regarded each other warily, flicking cautious knowing glances across the starched cloth and the Irish stew, glances that acknowl-edged our complicity in the final erasure of Mr Ryan.

Conspiracy, complicity; there is a queasy comfort to be taken from them, for they offer the shelter of the herd against the rampagings of the rogue.

But all the same my room seemed unusually bare and lonely that night, and I had the strange feeling that Mr Ryan's going had left a gap much larger than his presence could possibly have filled.

Hero

Summer, 1946.

He sat quietly on the beach, strong swimmer's shoulders slumped against the prop of an arm, long runner's legs folded neatly under him. His ruffled snuff-coloured hair, cropped short, was salt-bleached, and his face was heavy and angular, the twice-broken nose a focus for its hard planes, the eyes as grey as the sea that pounded towards the ebb. Behind him on the low bank sprawled the twisted windset trunks of trees, the scrawl of boobyalla, the green lushness of german ivy. Driftwood lay like old random bones on the beach and along the banks of the small creek that scoured the dun sand and slipped finally across the shallow bar into the strait.

The sand was bright still, the sea decorated by a small chop that had come up in the last hour. Earlier, while the sea had been calm, he had swum a mile out and back, taking pleasure in the hard trudging work, in the small strains imposed on his body. But with the tide beginning to set from the west, the wind rising outside the shelter of the cove where he sat and driving the short flat waves before it, it was no time to swim. So he sat, forty-one years old, content enough, beside his dark-haired wife and his gangling thirteen-year-old son, while in the open the wind and tide made a roughness of the sea that he did not much care for.

He picked idly at the maroon trunks with the white belt,

touched with a small private wryness the pale shrapnel scars on his legs, thinking of the morning a day away when he would drag on his Monday boots, smear his hair flat with Brylcreem, pull on the stained fedora, walk the half mile to the PMG lineyard. But, in the meantime, for this afternoon, he was at rest, private, relaxed.

The tide was beginning its strong swing along the coast, and the wind was picking up the short seas, churning a little sand off the point. The sun was lowering slowly, winding down the sky, and soon it would be time to go home. He delivered himself to thoughts of his thin-flanked wife, who would make love only at night.

It was the boy, idly tossing stones into the creek, who saw the man first. He was a long way out, opposite the point, an arm raised for a brief moment.

The boy called, and he stood up, frowning, to watch.

A quarter of a mile out, he thought, and the drift will take him further ... he's fighting the sea, the tide, trying to make the beach too soon. Stupid, he thought, wait, go with it, it'll land you a few miles further on, past the big bay ...

He could see that the man wasn't a strong swimmer.

And the sweep of the tide was taking him further out into the deep frightening bight of the bay ...

He stood, brushing sand from his trunks, watching for another sight of the tiny figure, the persistent semaphore of the pale and futile arm.

— Run, he said to the boy, run and tell the policeman, get the surf-boat out ... he's in trouble ...

Trouble, he thought, yes, he's in trouble all right ...

— I'd better go in after him, he said to his wife, and flexed his legs, his toes curling in the gritty sand.

He let his muscles slacken; it was as much preparation as he had time to make. He stood watching the water, knowing that he didn't want to go in there.

As he walked slowly down the beach he made the

necessary calculations: worked it out — how far, how long, where he would find the man in the naked grey hillocks. Because he knew that once he was in the water he would not be able to see him.

I can bring him in, he thought, a mile past the point, past the rocks, on that bad stony beach. If he's still there. If he doesn't panic, or tire too much. I just hope to Christ he doesn't try to grab me. I'll be tired by then ...

And: there's just the one place, and I've got to be sure of it, because it's the only place I'll find him ...

If I'm lucky ... and if he's lucky ...

Then it was too late for thinking that kind of thing, because the cold shallow water was splashing his ankles, and he made himself relax, loosening his solid muscles, knowing that the boat would be too late, that the tide was carrying the man too far, too fast. He wanted to run, but he made himself walk slowly through the shallows, letting the small vicious waves furl about his legs. He raised his knees high, feeling the cold water splash on the sun-warmed skin of his thighs. Thinking, it's a long way to walk ...

But it wasn't so far, and he was busy enough watching the short sharp waves as they came marching in their neat array.

And then the sea touched his groin, and he felt the sudden familiar shrinking. He dived, flat, easy, beginning the beat with his legs, making as much headway as he could before he had to come up for air.

Then he was in the chop, feeling the strong impersonal force of the tide and the waves. Not too bad, in so close. But there, all the same. His arms and shoulders were working, and his head was swinging in the breathing cycle, and he was riding the small pebble-hard waves. He rolled once on a crest, glanced at the cove. Saw his wife on the bare beach, solitary, complaisant; possessed, he thought, of more confidence than he had himself.

He turned back into the sea.

A long swim, he thought. Take it easy now, you'll need it all later … enough to get back. So he assaulted the powerful surge with moderation.

He settled into the old-fashioned crawl that worked so well and that took him strongly through the water, legs scissoring and beating and arms and shoulders working easily against the battering.

Hard, he thought, it'll be a hard one, the tide and the chop, and the distance, and all the way back … but it's better than a lot of things and more honest and once you start it's all right … it's always all right once you start, no matter what it is …

The water was very cold, and he thought, it's new water, pushed in from the southern ocean on top of the friendly water of the strait; and, breathing on a crest, reaching for more sea with his strong brown arms, he wondered again how long the man could last.

Oddly, he felt no urgency.

It was too far for that.

And he thought: let me get there before he gets too tired or too panicked, and — his mind bursting into sudden intemperance — God fuck you, let me get there, before the water takes him …

For some reason that he could not fathom, it mattered, it was important, that the man should sense someone else in the water with him, know that he was not alone.

Hang on, he thought … and didn't know why it suddenly seemed so urgent. But … hang on, he thought, hang on …

And the short hard chop began to batter at him, and he wished that it wasn't necessary to swim into it. He was well out now, and he knew from the short bruising strength of the sea that it was going to be very hard; felt the first small tremor of nervousness, because it was that much colder, that much more brutal, than he had expected. He let his long body flatten in the swimmer's private protection, felt his thigh muscles strong still, his knees locking firmly as he kicked.

And he thought, sliding through the grey water: better to think now of something else. Because it was beginning to frighten him a little.

A grey day, then — July, he remembered — and a threat of rain. The balcony of the police station, hurried linen banners. Heroes were in short supply in 1943, and even a noncom with an M.M. and a Mention in Despatches was worth a Saturday afternoon. And: stuff the M.M., but I earned the Mention, he thought, that last nasty half mile along the wire with the shells bursting too bloody close ...

And the old boy had made a speech ... ex-Oxford, Rhodes Scholar, had always liked him because he could bowl his thirty overs, kick a ball seventy yards, take a punch ... The rest ... well, nothing but feet, because he had refused to look at the faces that grey day ... there were too many with a strange softness in their eyes ... but his wife had been pleased ... heroes are good for a day, at least, he thought without bitterness.

He realized that there was little hope for the man. Too far, too hard ...

But still, there was, there *must* be hope ... let him who is without hope among you sink to the bottom ...

He knew that *that* wasn't right. And brought his head back into the sea. It was taking him, turning him, moving him with the drift. Christ, he thought, if I could turn a little, go with it, I could swim till next Shrove Tuesday ... have to turn a little, face the chop head-on, swim for that spot where he might be ...

So he turned a little to his left, taking the chop in his face.

A break. Dive, let his body go deep, and suddenly all the fury was gone. No air, but rest for a little. Above him the short waves still crashed.

And the night of the reception ... nowhere to sleep ...

plenty of cheers in the afternoon, but when darkness and rain came and cold, no bloody room at the inn ... and he was surprised at the bitterness in himself ...

In the end they had found two leaky makeshift rooms on the verandah of an old boarding house ... and his son waking in the night, afraid ...

Fuck you all, he thought, fuck you all ...

He surfaced, and felt the chop begin to take him, to beat at him, and that special spot in the sea seemed impossibly distant ... but he was sure that he would reach that small patch of bare sea, would arrive there, somehow. And maybe, he thought, I won't be alone, there's always the chance ...

He picked one of the occasional big waves and swam strongly up on its crest, looked out to sea as his head came clear.

But there was nothing.

Only the sea.

It's a mile, he thought, it must be a mile ...

And: heroes go cheap ... banners are fine and speeches and free drinks for an afternoon and lamingtons and tea and we're winning the war ... but four years was enough and he was thirty-eight and he had his scars and all he wanted was a job ... full employment, but they all looked the other way, all the ones who had stayed at home. So there was the lineyard, and £4/7/6 a week and four moves from house to rented house in the last three years ...

He's out there, he thought, and let them all write him off, but even if he's got to die, well, it's important, it's *necessary*, that he doesn't die on his own ...

He began to feel afraid then. Not of what the sea was doing to him — he was still swimming strongly — but at what it *could* do to him, *would* do. Because the chop, angling across the tide-set, was starting to tire him, starting to break the rhythm of his stroke a little. He found that it was harder to breathe cleanly, and he was swallowing a little water.

He took another spell, sunk himself again and when his lungs at last demanded air he porpoised up, and there was only water and more water, and he drove harder with his legs and the air was mixed with froth and spume, and he took it, knowing that he was swallowing water. He must watch for cramps now, he thought, and that heaviness in the gut. But he had not taken much water in his lungs, and that was good. He butted into the chop, swinging his head a little farther on the breathing strokes.

It's going to get harder, he thought, and took no comfort from the knowledge.

You go into the RSL, he thought, because people pressure you, and because you've got a few mates there, and because there's nowhere else to go, and you drink a bit too much ... but that little man that went round touching people, Christ, I wasn't under control then, not really, I'd say fine, don't let it get to you ... and then one day ... all the savagery ... I turned round and I was ready to kill him ... but someone who knew about it all stopped me and the little man went away ... but it takes the shine off ...

If only I was twenty again, he thought. But at least I'm still swimming ...

The water was colder now, cold with the chill of the big casual brutal ocean. But his ankle was fine, and the cold wasn't hurting any more, the early stiffness was gone. There was the accustomed abiding coldness from the metal fragment in his knee, but he was used to that. He was all right.

But he wasn't all right, because the sea had taken away the smoothness of his stroke and left him with a slightly jagged rhythm that wasn't quite good enough. And he was aware of it.

He took another rest, then, and at the end of it, coming

untidily up from it he still could not see the special spot, and thought, I'm not sure of anything anymore ...

Then he began to vomit a little, and took another quick rest under the waves.

But he made it a short one, pushed himself back into the punishment of the chop.

I'm getting hurt, he thought, this bloody chop is damaging me. But still, I'm making progress, moving forward, out, out towards that spot.

He didn't dare think of the swim back.

Swim, he told himself, vomiting on the outbreath, sucking too hard on the inbreath. Swim, bugger you, swim ...

Taking another rest, lying in the calm below the roiling surface, deep, bereft of air, but intact, he thought: I can't take too much of this ... no, no, I suppose I can take as much as I have to ... but it's bad stuff ...

If I could only see, I'm too low in the water ... and I'm taking a bit of a belting ...

He went on swimming, butting into the shoulders of the sea.

I'm not making much headway, he thought, and realized that he had swallowed too much water and that his body was curling forward in a gentle arc, that the sea was defeating the flat athlete's body that had always been his pride. My guts, he thought, all that water in my guts ... A dull pain, and he accepted it at last, checked his stroke and made the small adjustments. But he found that his back muscles were aching too badly, and his thighs, and that his arms were trying to compensate ... so he locked his knees again, drove on, the grey sea solid against him, a wall that met him, gave him its regular blows. He wished again that he could turn and swim with it, let it wash over his shoulders, breathe in the small troughs. But not yet ...

He concentrated on his knees, made them lock, drove himself harder, tighter, stronger, into the stiff thudding seas. And realized with a dull despair that he wasn't moving forward now, but was losing ground …

Then, miraculously, he passed the edge of his exhaustion and felt the lift of a renewed drive, a second wind, and swam on, churning hard and strong. He was swimming well now and his tiredness was gone and he butted further out into the strait. And his knees were working properly and his strokes were measured by the small circuits in his head and when he took a rest it was only a short one. He would lie beneath the confusion of the surface and look downward and watch the bottom, the grey-white sand silent and smooth thirty fathoms beneath him.

And then he felt it going again, felt the strength ebbing, felt it worse now, because he was losing his grip on the water, his hands were opening, the fingers splaying. He said in his head the few small curses that he allowed himself, cupped his hands, tried to lock his knees at the proper part of the beat, but he knew that his legs were going, that his arms were taking too much of the strain, and that the frequent rests he took, deep under the waves, were not bringing back his strength, but only holding him in a kind of static exhaustion. And he despised for a little his ageing and inadequate body. But he went on using it as best he could, crashing up through the broken water, trudging slowly and bitterly along his invisible path.

His mind seemed full of strange shattered images. I could do with a beer, he thought. Feeling the heaviness in his muscles he knew that his body had reached the point where the technique of swimming was diminished, almost gone, and that from now on it would be no more than slogging, of forcing his protesting body past old limits. And he thought then, fighting himself as well as the sea, of John Dunn. Change places with you, mate, he thought.

And! No, no mate of mine, fuck you …

He lay deep in the water, limply, thinking, maybe the boat ... letting the sea move easily about him. And thinking, I'm bloody exhausted now, it's been too hard, I'm like a bloody boxer, out on my feet ... and there'll be no boat ...

He was losing ground again, the sea beating him back. So he swung into it again, butting wearily forward.

And thinking, my legs are buggered, now it's all on my shoulders ... And why did I think of John Dunn? ... Well, he thought, once you start on something ... and I let in all that about the RSL ... and it's a kind of chain ...

... walking up the long polished bar in the evening, still in his work clothes, his haversack slung across his shoulder ... and there at the small table in the corner, there was Dunny in his blue suit, a director in the family company. He'd had no wish to join him, but spoke: Hello John. After all, first names for three years and it had never occurred to him that it might be any different from the Libyan desert ... and John had smiled at him a little oddly and said: Captain Dunn, if you don't mind ... and Perry Andrews had come over and touched his arm and said: Don't worry Harry, the world's full of shits ... but he'd finished his beer and walked out and never gone back and that had been the end of something ...

Christ, he thought, suddenly, I must be there, I must be in the right place ... I don't know how I know, but I *do* ... I'm *there* ... drift and current and tide and speed and all the small important things that added up ...

Now, he thought, I have to find him, if he's still above water, and get him back ...

And: Fuck you, John Dunn, but I'd still change places with you, whatever you're doing, wherever you are ...

Then: No I wouldn't, because you're a different kind of bastard altogether ...

And: I have to get back ...

I'm very tired now, he thought ... but at least I can turn

soon … swim with it … a long way … but … where was I?

His eyes were sore and salt-stung. He squinted hard. Well, he thought, at least I'm still on top of the water, I'm a bit wrecked, but from now on … soon … just a plain old slog …

And: He's gone, I'm too late, he's never made it, or else he's down there in the quiet under the waves, rolling and dead and there's nothing I can do. But this is the right place …

So he turned in the water and looked as well as he could. He picked a wave and rode it up and looked again. Christ, he thought, I can't swim back over *this* place … I can't even look for him, not properly … but at least he must have known that I was *coming* … so even though I didn't make it, he wasn't alone, because *someone* was trying…

I've done all I can, he decided. And because there was nothing else left to do he turned away, racked and half-suffocated and very near the end of his own strength and no longer really sure of anything, not even where the land lay. But, he thought, if I take the chop on my right shoulder…

And so he began the long swim back.

The sea still beat at him, and now it tried to turn him out into the strait; but breathing was easier, so much easier, and his useless legs didn't worry him too much, and if his fingers were splaying again there was nothing he could do about *that* … so he fought on blindly, making a little headway, helped by the tide, drawing on the last of his strength and endurance and finding it barely enough … but swimming, swimming still …

He vomited every few strokes now and his vision seemed oddly red and tunneled. But he went on, his movements clumsy and ragged, only half co-ordinated, riding the energy of the tide and wind and following sea.

I'm buggered, he thought, finding his hands too often empty when he stroked, I'm buggered ...

And his mind began to grow increasingly vacant, like the empty convolutions of a sea-washed shell.

The sun was low enough to paint deep shadows on the ochre of the rocks of the point. But he did not see them. He sensed, though, the lessening of the sea's tension and knew that he had passed the finger of the promontory. He dug deeper, pulled himself somehow towards the beach. And came ashore in the late afternoon on the flat plain of the beach. The tide was at full ebb, the sand stippled darkly with small sharp rocks. He took cuts from them on his knees and elbows and hands as he floundered in the shallows.

The sea released him at last, rolled him to the tide-edge where he lay trying with almost the last of his strength to keep his face out of the wash. He stood up somehow, staggered a few paces, unable to control the trembling in his leg muscles; fell, stood again, staggered higher up the beach. The line of boobyallas seemed faint and wavering. Then he could no longer stagger, so he crawled for a little, thinking, Oh, Christ I'm thirsty ...

Finally he let his body collapse on the still-warm sand, the coarse grains mottling his wet skin. He was very cold, but mostly thirsty and he didn't want to move at all. And fragments of broken thought rose to the surface of his mind: What day is it? ... And what in Christ is it all about? ...

And: ... of course ... just so that someone mustn't ... mustn't feel *abandoned* at the end ... but I'm not sure I'll be able to tell anyone why ... ever ...

He lay very still, too exhausted to move again, and let the flat sunlight begin to dry his twitching skin.

And then, after what seemed a very long time, he allowed himself to faint.

Right of Way

Milking is over. The seventy-three Friesians, slack-uddered, mill aimlessly for a little then head off down the rutted track towards the lower pasture. I watch as Reg and Peter clean up, follow them as they clump into the kitchen. The room seems suddenly filled with loud boots and cow smells. Amy opens the oven door, takes out the joint, begins to drain vegetables. Reg, still damp from a quick wash, carves. Outside the window the light is fading and the wide garden is filled with shadows. There is an autumn chill to the air, and the warmth of the room is welcome.

We begin to eat. I have done little enough during my visit, but I eat as much, and with as much gusto, as the others.

His first hunger blunted, Reg looks across the table at Peter. 'We'd better order the trees for the new wind-break…'

Peter, chewing, nods. 'Should get some rain soon … then we can stop carting irrigation pipes and get the planting done …'

The two of them are very much alike. Peter, at twenty-five, is short, broad, bearded, with a lean-boned obstinate face. But instead of his father's blue eyes he has Amy's brown ones, and his beard — as full as Reg's — is deep brown, unstreaked with grey.

Amy begins to serve the rhubarb pie. 'What are you going to plant?'

'Horizontalis,' says Reg.

'Torulosa,' says Peter.

Blue eyes lock with brown.

'Horizontalis ...'

'Torulosa ...'

I sense the sudden tension. It is odd, unusual. They are a close-knit family, and I had thought the work of the farm too familiar, too ingrained, for questions of authority to rise. And there is nothing of the patriarch in Reg.

'Well ...' says Amy.

'Forget about torulosa,' says Reg. 'They'd take too long to fill the gaps ...'

'That ridge is dry,' says Peter. 'Plant horizontalis you'll end up with die-back ...'

'Horizontalis,' says Reg, glaring hard at the mustard pot.

'Torulosa,' says Peter, eyes fixed on the sugar bowl.

Reg stands up suddenly, leaving his pie half-eaten, and walks wordlessly out of the kitchen. In a moment Peter gets up too, goes out by the other door. From the small room next door that serves as an office come the sounds of Reg rummaging through papers, rattling drawers, muttering. Outside, the light goes on in the garage and there is a clatter of tools as Peter does violent things to the tractor.

Amy and I sit silently at the table, finish our pie, drink our tea. She is smiling a little. She catches my glance, sees that I'm uneasy. 'Don't worry,' she says, 'they'll work it out. Eventually ...'

But the next day sees no resolutions. How can there be resolution? There is no discussion, barely even speech. Reg and Peter go about the jobs of the farm grunting a minimum of monosyllables. The second day is the same. I feel more and more uncomfortable, think about bringing my visit to an early end. But Amy seems unworried. In fact she has an air of quiet amusement. At least when the two men are absent. So I stick it, although it all seems quite ridiculous ... a windbreak, a row of trees on an exposed hillside, a few dozen cypresses or whatever ... and they're at war: silent, stubborn, hostile.

Another day passes. No change.

In the afternoon I help them shift the irrigation pipes. I drive the truck round the paddocks — at least I can do that — while Reg and Peter walk alongside, still silent and grim, tossing up the pipes. We finish late in the afternoon, set up the tractor and pump at a new spot, go back to the house to get ready for milking.

Peter climbs into the cab of the old Bedford. 'Goin' to move the fence ...' He means, I suppose, the electric fencing in the pasture on the other side of the creek. Reg says nothing, stumps into the kitchen for a cup of tea. I follow him in and he smiles at me, suddenly, almost apologetically, as if aware of the childishness of their behaviour. But he says nothing. And neither do I. We are good friends, but not old ones. And what can I say, anyway?

We sit at the table, with Amy, drinking tea. Through the window we can see the fall of the land, the long winding track that leads over the hillside and down to the creek. As we watch, the brown truck comes into view, crawling down the track.

'There's Clayton,' says Reg suddenly, and gets up and goes to the window. And I see a red tractor moving slowly down the other side of the valley. Like Peter, Clayton is heading for the bridge over the creek.

I have never met Clayton, but he is a sore subject with Reg and Peter. A neighbour for thirty years, but not a friend. Too many small things have mounted up. Brush fires too near boundary fences, gates left open, promises unkept. And finally the house on the hill. It has been pointed out to me, the house. A year or two ago Clayton decided to build a new house on top of the ridge to the north. He did it, too, hacked out a great clearing in the bush and built a monstrous square brick barn there. Reg and Peter resent it. The long line of the ridge has been denuded at its highest point, scarred like the spine of a dog with mange. The skyline of free tall bush that they have enjoyed all their lives has been fractured. Nothing to be done, it is Clayton's land. His bush, his trees.

But their skyline.

Then, of course, there's the right of way. Clayton's property sweeps round Reg's in a great arc, and the narrow neck where the bridge crosses the creek is a natural road for Clayton when he wants to go from the north to the south pastures of his land. He *can* go the other way. But he has always kept the right of way open, even when he doesn't really need it. A matter of principle. When the old bridge was damaged last year by the floods, though, he refused to pay his share in the cost of replacing it. Reg and Peter built a new concrete bridge and paid for it themselves. And Clayton, of course, uses the new bridge, just as he did the old. The right of way must be kept open.

So now we watch with interest as Clayton's red tractor descends the slope on one side of the creek, Peter's truck on the other. There is a strange inevitability about it. We are aware, I think, even when they are separated by half a mile, that they will meet at the bridge.

And of course they do. Not only at the bridge, but on it, in the very middle.

We watch, waiting for one of them to back up, to let the other pass.

But neither does. The two vehicles sit, bonnets almost touching, three feet above the run of clear brown water. The sun is dropping towards the hills now, and the light flashes redly on the tractor's paintwork. As far as we can tell, neither of them has said anything. They both just sit silently, stubbornly. Waiting.

Reg gets up, opens the window, cocks his head. 'Peter's switched off his engine ...'

In a moment or two we hear the tractor's engine stop too. Reg smiles a little to himself. Sits down, drinks his tea, smokes a cigarette, watches the static scene on the bridge. The sun is touching the tips of the western hills now, and the valley, the creek and bridge, are in shadow. There is no movement.

'You better give us a hand with the milking,' says Reg, to Amy, getting up. Considerately, he doesn't suggest that I help. He knows I'd be worse than useless. I stay in the kitchen, peel vegetables, make sure the stew doesn't burn. And watch the creek and the two vehicles nose to nose in the fading light.

By the time the milking is finished I can barely see the creek, the bridge, the vehicles. But they are still there, unmoving, locked in their strange and silent confrontation. It must be cold down there, I think, and Peter is in his shirt-sleeves.

Reg and Amy come back into the kitchen. Reg eats his meal in silence, sits smoking cigarette after cigarette. It is quite dark outside now, and the stars are bright and cold; there is more than a hint of frost in the air.

At last, suddenly decisive, Reg stands up. 'Want to come for a walk?' he asks me.

I get up, put on a jacket.

Side by side we walk down the hill, stumbling a little in the darkness over the rocks and ruts. Reg doesn't say anything.

We come out onto the flat by the creek, walk along beside the willows that line the bank. By the water, down in the valley, it seems even colder.

Suddenly we are at the bridge. I nearly run into the tray of the Bedford. We walk round the side to the cab. A few feet away I can see the tractor, colourless now in the dark. The bonnet is already bloomed with dew. I can see, beyond the steering wheel, the faint outline of a hatted head, hoary puffs of breath.

Reg wrenches open the truck door, looks up at Peter. 'Go and have your tea,' he says. 'I'll take over...'

Wordlessly Peter climbs down, shivering, and Reg jumps up, settles into the driver's seat. Slams the door. Sits glaring through the windscreen at the barely visible Clayton.

Peter and I trudge back up the track towards the lights of the house. Halfway up the hill he starts to laugh quietly. By the time we reach the house we are both laughing, roaring, convulsed.

Peter eats his meal, showers, and we sit at the table to wait.

It is a long wait.

But at last it ends. The clock shows ten past eleven when we hear the sudden cough of an engine from the valley, clear in the cold air, I can see a dim glow that looks like torchlight. Peter relaxes, grins. The sound of the tractor engine mounts, revving, then slowly fades. We have to wait for a few minutes before we hear the motor of the Bedford grind to life. We can see the headlights cutting crazy patterns through the willows as Reg backs and fills. Finally the lights steady and the truck begins to climb the hill.

A few minutes later the truck pulls up outside. Reg comes into the kitchen, grinning fiercely, rubbing his hands. He stands over the stove, stamping and chafing. Amy pours him a cup of tea, and he sits down at the table with us.

No one says anything about Clayton.

'We'll order those trees tomorrow,' says Reg.

'What sort?' asks Peter, slyly.

'I thought we might give those golden Brunnianas a try ...' Reg looks innocently across the table at him.

'Yeah, why not,' says Peter. 'They'll give the old place a bit of colour, anyway. Liven it up a bit ...'

We all have another cup of tea.

The Last Compartment

At the end of summer Olwen, newly widowed, left the city and moved into an old farmhouse a mile from the Laceys' ten acres.

In the blustering uncertainties of autumn, Richard Lacey bought the railway carriage.

During the weeks before delivery of the carriage Richard spent much of his time justifying his purchase to Nella, his wife; it would be an adjunct to the pottery; a storage shed; an essay in conceptual art. His production of handthrown dinner-services fell off, and the household suffered temporary cash-flow difficulties. But Nella — dark, thin, sardonic — said nothing, knowing that silence was the quickest road to a resumption of production.

Olwen visited them several times. 'We were at school together, you know,' said Richard, as they watched Olwen's departing figure — full-bodied, erect, high-breasted, the long blonde hair ruffled by the wind — after one of her visits.

'You told me,' said Nella.

'We were never close, though ...'

'You mean you never screwed her.'

'What a nasty mind you've got.' He smoothed back his dark receding hair and stalked off, a little plump now in his thirty-ninth year, towards the pottery. Nella turned away, climbed into the car to fetch their daughter Karen from school. During the drive it occurred to her that

Richard had not mentioned the imminent arrival of the carriage to Olwen.

'Right, mate,' said the truck-driver. 'Where do you want her?'

The truck bearing the carriage had arrived finally, labouring up the narrow gravel road, a heavy crane trundling behind.

Richard stood staring up in rapt euphoria at the long body of the carriage, its green sheen dulled by the coating of white dust. He climbed to the running-board, hung there fondling the heavy bloomed-brass loop of a door-handle, craning to peer through an opaque window.

'Well, mate?'

'Oh.' Richard jumped clumsily down. 'Up there. Behind the trees.' He led the way into the tall thicket behind the pottery. Creosoted sleepers bridged heavy concrete stumps.

The driver was puzzled. 'What you want it up there for?'

Richard was patient. 'Because this way it will be just the right height from the ground. Just as if it was still on wheels, on the tracks ...'

Nella, watching quizzically, realized then that it might be something more than an extra toolshed, an exercise in conceptual art.

The exact height from the tracks?

By evening the carriage rested on its final plinth behind the screen of gums and wattles. Richard ate hurriedly, rushed back to open doors, to raise and lower windows, to test the ancient cracked leather of the seats.

Nella had followed him, stood looking up, ignored. She seemed to sense a certain resentment at her presence.

Karen, nine, still in her brown school uniform, joined her. They stood watching silently for a time, but in the face of his studied indifference finally left.

Later, preparing for bed, Nella asked him, 'How much did you pay for it?'

'You know that ... a hundred dollars.'

'Yes, but what about the cartage and all that?'

He was silent for a moment, folding his jeans. Then, 'Another hundred or so ...'

'And what,' she said from between the sheets, 'was all that about getting it just the right height?'

He slipped into bed, turned his back, switched off the light. 'If you're doing something you might as well do it right.'

In a minute or so his voice came again, a little muffled, shaded with a curious tentative quality. 'Don't tell Olwen about it ...'

She was so startled that she said nothing. But she lay for a long time listening to his snoring, wondering.

He was gone from the bed when she woke. She slipped on an old sweater and jeans, left the house, climbed the track past the pottery. A heavy foreign door slammed among the gum trees, and she trod more quietly, stood at the edge of the small clearing looking at the carriage. Flat early sunlight lit lustrous green smears on the old panelling where hands, slings, fingers, had drawn random graffiti in the dust. She could not see Richard, but there were muted sounds from within the long green body.

Shivering in the early chill, she felt a small unease at the sight of the alien object planted so arbitrarily in the bush; its antique blockiness, its obsolete stolidity. There was a wrongness to it, she knew; a train was for journeys, for directions, and this relic was anchored now for ever, rooted among stringybark, silver wattle, manfern and prickly mimosa. There was a sadness, too, at the prospect of windows past which the landscape would never flow again.

She caught sight of his flushed unshaven face at the

window. For a moment he said nothing. Then, grudgingly, 'Well, you want to come and look?'

She picked her way slowly to the running-board, climbed up. It was one of the middle compartments, and she looked about curiously. Ten years younger than Richard, she had never seen such a thing before, let alone ridden in one.

The leather seats had only a rip or two, the varnished panels were only slightly gouged. A pane of glass that covered one of the photographs above the seats was cracked. The photographs themselves were faded to a mellow uniform sepia that left only a hint of the antique views.

'How many compartments are there?' she asked.

'Eight,' he said. 'The ones with bogs only had six.'

She looked once more about her. There seemed nothing more to see. 'I've got to get Karen out of bed, she'll be late for school ...' She fumbled with the heavy door.

Walking back down the track she thought — with light cynicism — that whatever Richard had in mind for the carriage it would not be utilitarian.

In the afternoon, she herded him, unwilling, to the pottery, to work. Watching him slam clay onto the wheel with sharp impatience, she remembered what he had said the night before.

Don't tell Olwen ...

So of course she would, at the earliest opportunity.

She invited Olwen to afternoon tea, watched the older woman carefully. There was an air of quiet steadiness about her. The blue eyes were widespread, with the light of some humour that lay oddly with the slight sulkiness of the heavy mouth.

'Come for a walk,' said Nella when they had finished their tea. 'I've got something to show you.'

Walking along the track, Olwen looked about her at the

land. 'I envy you,' she said. 'It's lovely.' She paused. 'You're both lucky. I was a country kid, but I've lived in cities ever since school.' She paused again. 'Richard and I were at school together, did you know?'

'I know,' said Nella, noncommittally.

Then suddenly they were past the screening brush, and the carriage stood before them. Nella noticed that Richard had wiped away the dust, and the carriage seemed even stranger now, its smooth brightness outlandish among the dull olives of the autumn bush.

They stopped.

She looked at Olwen, but the placid face was expressionless, unrevealing.

'Richard bought it,' said Nella. 'I thought you might be interested.'

Olwen was silent for a moment. Then, 'It's the sort they had on the trains we went to high school in every day ...'

Nella waited, but Olwen said no more, showed no signs of wanting to approach the carriage more closely.

They walked back down the track in silence.

'What are you doing?' she asked.

'Lights,' said Richard, strung with wires, high on a ladder wedged in a treefork. 'Need lights if it's going to be any use ...'

At the end of a week the small bulbs behind their thick glass domes were lit for the first time in perhaps twenty years. She saw the dim glow through the trees, and went to look. The carriage was a dark bulk against the night, pasted with the rectangles of yellow windows.

She discovered him one day in the living room occupied with the tape deck. Seeing her, he quickly turned down the volume to a low murmur. But it was too late. She picked up a tape, another: *Southern Steam, Sounds of British Rail, Steam Trains of the World ...*

'What are they for?'

'What do you bloody think? To listen to ...'

The spare speakers disappeared, the old tape deck and amplifier.

She held her peace; puzzled, only mildly concerned.

But as the days turned to weeks, and as Richard disappeared at night with greater and greater regularity, her small concern grew, spread, filled more and more of the spaces of her mind. And it was not the absences themselves which worried her; it was something odd about their character. For they seemed to have taken on a compulsive and secretive aspect. And now he actively discouraged her occasional visits to the carriage.

Visiting Olwen, Nella one day raised again the question of the carriage. 'Why do you think he doesn't want you to know?'

Olwen hesitated. When she spoke her voice carried an unaccustomed uncertainty. 'You know Richard hates me, don't you?'

'Hates you?' Nella was startled. 'Surely not? He often used to tell me how long you'd known each other, all the way from kindergarten through high school ...'

'Yes ...' Then, 'You know we used to travel to school by train, don't you?'

Nella nodded. 'But what's that got to do with the carriage? There's no harm in it, surely?'

'No? Perhaps not ...'

And that was all she would say.

Richard swept, dusted, oiled door hinges. But his restoration of the carriage was limited to little more than housekeeping. And — when Nella was not at home — he spent long hours with tape deck, splicer and stopwatch.

At night he sat in the first, the rear compartment. The switches were there, and besides, it was where he had usually travelled in those other days.

He would sit, eyes closed, ears tuned only to the sounds from the speakers recreating the trip he had made so many times in those five years. The echoing platform of the dim station, the slippage as the pistons turned the six big driving wheels of the old DS engine; the slow crawl to the first crossing, the high hoarse scream of the whistle; then the slowly increasing tempo through the outskirts of the town, the quickening chuff as the driver opened the regulator when they swung down onto the flats towards the first river; fast, fast, the old carriages rattling, tocking over the points.

And sometimes, sometimes, he would almost catch it, despite the stillness beneath his buttocks. But the veracity of the tape's orchestration itself would betray him, and he would open his eyes. And — instead of the flying shadows, the pastures and clearings flung with rushing light — there would be only the still dark bush, familiar and unresponsive.

But he continued, all the same, night after night; hoping for miracles he could not even define ...

One night, though, disillusioned a little in the strengthening gales of late autumn, he lowered a window, leaned out.

And at once a great thrust of emotion seized and shook him. For the wild gusts from the north-west, rushing past the train, seemed not a simple equinoctial gale, but the wind of the train's own passage through darkness, through wild and uncertain dreams.

That night, lying beside the sleeping Nella, he realized for the first time, that — inexplicably — he had programmed not the outward morning journey, but the return voyage that had carried him through the electric darkness.

Darkness, and those nights in the last year of high school. The late train, forbidden to all except the athletes who stayed behind for practice. There were few of them — himself, Olwen, a handful of others — and they had scattered, usually, spread themselves over the length of the train. Why, he sometimes wondered, didn't they congregate? They seldom did, that was all he knew. Perhaps, like him at seventeen, the darkness, the aloneness had sparked in them strange dreams and fantasies.

He sat, when he could, alone in the rear compartment of the last carriage. There was purpose here, and sometimes his courage was equal to it. And even at the beginning, perhaps, there was buried in his mind the seed of a project so desperate that it might not be consciously contemplated.

He began, tentatively at first, and snail-paced, to travel within the static confines of the train's speed, as a fly may crawl upon the windscreen of a racing car. Certain conditions were necessary. It was essential that he move on the right-hand side of the train. For he knew, after four years of daily travel, that the old DS engines had at least one unique feature: the driver's post was at the left. So it was necessary to move on the other side. And the guard might at any moment glance the length of the train. So travel was safe only when the train was moving through a left-hand bend, and he was concealed by the bulging curve of carriages.

At first he moved cautiously, nervously, deathly afraid of the rattling wheels a yard below him as he wormed his way out through one window and into the next. For a time he restricted himself to movement between a single pair of compartments. But later he grew bolder, extended his voyages, learned to carry his Gladstone bag slung on a string across his back, travelled the length of three, four, even five compartments.

At the icy nadir of winter he traversed, one freezing night, a whole eight-compartmented carriage and returned to disembark soberly — if grubbily — from his original dog-box.

He never attempted to move from one carriage to

another. One world seemed to satisfy him. And in a while his ardour abated a little. But all the same, he felt a strange and excited impatience growing in him. He became concerned with seating arrangements in other carriages. Found himself watching carefully the choices of the other travellers, mounting to his own compartment only when all the others were seated. Remaining always alone, burning with a strange uneasiness.

Waiting.

Nella, patient in her sheepskin jacket, sitting on a stump, watched each night. In the beginning she was amused, despite Richard's long periods of inactivity. For on some nights he would not move at all. Except perhaps to open a window, let the wind beat in his face, tear at his sparse hair. Then the window would be closed again, the wooden-louvred shutters drawn up, the compartment sealed.

On other nights, though, when the wind was strong and the soundtrack loud, the window at the back of the carriages would open and Richard, an old Gladstone bag — she couldn't think where he had found it — slung over his shoulder by a cord, would writhe laboriously through the opening and struggle into the window of the next compartment. Sometimes he would advance the length of several compartments; sometimes return, sometimes not. But she noticed that he never moved far beyond the middle of the carriage, the fourth or fifth compartment.

She could always tell when it was time to go. The soundtrack told her. For it was never repeated, replayed, on any single night. And when the sound of slowing wheels, the reluctance of hoarse pistons, the last of the signal whistles came, she knew that it was time to slip away.

By the time Richard reached the bedroom she was always tucked snugly in the high brass bed, pretending sleep.

Nella returned to her inquisition of Olwen while they were driving to a meeting of the local repertory society.

'Did the boys and girls travel together on the train? When you and Richard went to school?'

Olwen shook her head. 'You know what boys are at that age … dirty little beasts.'

'Dirty?'

'Well, apart from sex … filthy, you know, shitting on bits of paper and leaving it under the seats …'

'How horrible …' Then, 'But didn't you sometimes travel with the boys? I mean, Richard's told me about the late train. And you were older then, almost adults …'

'Sometimes.' Olwen's smile was a little thin, impatient. 'But generally … oh, they were such drags, so I used to wait till everyone was settled, then find an empty compartment. There were never many other passengers. The engine used to pull up near the station lavatory, so I hid there and waited. I used to end up mostly in the front carriage.'

Letting Olwen out at her gate, she said, 'You remember you said that Richard hated you? I'm sure you're wrong — to tell the truth, I think he finds you very attractive …'

Olwen laughed a little sharply. 'He had a crush on me for years, at school, but I couldn't stand him. You know how they are at that age …' Her smile softened a little. 'Don't worry, I'm no threat to you …'

They both laughed. But as Nella drove away she realized that Olwen had not really answered her.

But Nella was a patient woman, and she knew that sooner or later she would find out the truth.

A fortnight later the opportunity came at a neighbour's party. Richard, loud on red wine, was snared in public argument, and Nella found herself isolated with Olwen in a conversational backwater.

She declined equivocation. 'There was more to it than

just a crush, wasn't there?' she said, smiling her sardonic smile. 'With you and Richard?'

After a little wine Olwen seemed less reticent than usual. 'Oh, well ...'

'Come on,' said Nella, 'tell!'

Olwen shrugged, lit a cigarette. 'Well, yes, it *was* more than just a crush, I suppose. And it went on for years. But I just couldn't *stand* him! Not that there was anything *wrong* with him, it was just, you know, the chemistry ...'

'He's very persistent', said Nella, prompting.

Olwen was silent.

'The train,' said Nella, 'it was something to do with the train, wasn't it?'

Olwen hesitated. 'I did something very bad to him, I've never really forgiven myself ...'

'You? To Richard? I don't believe it ...'

'No, really, it was something quite bad, cruel.' Olwen watched the smoking end of her cigarette.

'Richard buying that carriage,' said Nella, 'it had something to do with you coming to live out here, didn't it?'

'I hope not,' said Olwen, and she seemed suddenly very sober.

The silence lengthened.

'You know,' said Olwen at last, 'he used to crawl along the train, in and out of windows. On the trip home at night. He thought no one knew, but of course everyone did. It's strange,' she said. 'Usually kids would boast about it. But there was something different about this, something not quite — right.'

'I'll guess,' said Nella, eyes dancing with quiet malice. 'One night he crawled in *your* window, didn't he?'

Olwen's blue eyes flickered at her. She nodded.

'What happened?'

'Oh Christ,' said Olwen, 'it was awful, so bloody awful ...'

She took several deep drags at her cigarette, stubbed it

out, went on in a sudden rush of words. 'It was only a few minutes after we left the station. I was in the front compartment, sitting there reading, facing the engine, and the window on the other side of the carriage rattled, dropped open, and he climbed in. He had that silly bag hung round his neck, and he was all flushed and sweaty, covered in grit. He just stood there for a minute, staring at me, looking silly. Half embarrassed, half aggressive. Then, suddenly, without a word, he unbuttoned his fly and … you know, took it out.' She giggled a little, a strange, half-apologetic giggle. 'He was — you know — all ready for action. I'd grown up in a houseful of brothers, so I knew all about it, but in those days, well, I just didn't *do* it …'

Nella's amber eyes were as bright, as voracious as a starling's. 'Go on — what happened?'

'Oh,' said Olwen, 'I was very blasé in those days, very … you know, sophisticated. I used to *smoke*! Anyway, there I was, sitting in my school uniform, and there *he* was, half out of his. So I just put on this really cool look — you know — and lit a cigarette. I looked right at his fly, at *it* … And I said to him, really *bored* I said, "Oh Richard, do put it away, you look so silly!" He just gaped at me, his face getting redder and redder, his thing sticking out. Then I did this awful thing.' She paused. 'I took a big lungful of smoke, and blew it on his thing. Then I just opened my book again and ignored him. But I could see from the corner of my eye, he just stood there *shrivelling* … Then, after a while he sat down in the corner, as far away from me as he could get, buttoned himself up and stared out the window all the way home. Never said a word. And when the train stopped, he just threw open the door and *bolted* …'

'I think you were bloody marvellous,' said Nella, silent screams of laughter racing deliciously through the conduits of her body. 'Bloody marvellous!'

And she began to have some inkling of what fantasies

might be germinating in the long procession of nights in the carriage, in the mind she had thought she knew so well.

'Actually,' said Olwen, 'the longer I think about it, the more I'm convinced I behaved like an absolute arse-hole...'

Richard had found it impossible to duplicate exactly the sounds of the night's journey. But his approximations were close, and closing his eyes he felt the geography of his fantasy assuming greater and greater solidity. And on certain nights when the seasonal gales racked the valley, roared through the clearing, tossed the wild plumes of the gum trees, he fancied almost that he felt the movements — the rockings, rattlings, creakings — of invisible motion.

As winter deepened, cold companion to his engross-ment, he felt a growing expectation. And although his journeys never took him as far as the last compartment, its presence loomed more and more enticingly, immanent and summoning in the chill darkness.

He was conscious of a waiting; but for what he could not admit, could not even define. But it occurred to him that Olwen was herself involved somehow in the waiting, and with a patience perhaps even greater than his own. The thought of her began to occupy more and more of the long hours of his immobility; and he found at last that cer-tain trembling admissions had risen without his bidding, even his knowledge. For he knew that he had never hated her, only his own ineptitude; was certain that it was he — and never, never she — who was to blame for his destruc-tion.

Decisions can be delayed, deferred. But finally, on a night when the train seemed to plunge and buck through the great winds of the night, he realized that exorcism could be delayed no longer. He sat for a few short minutes, the bag ready slung, knowing that he must act. Then, as the whistle heralded the beginning of the open country, the long curve of the first left-hand bend, the full weight of necessity descended finally upon him.

As new wine fills an old dry flask, so he was filled with tremors of excitement, expectancy, apprehension; and a strange, almost sad, lust.

He climbed, deliberately, slowly, out through the window, progressed with practised ease towards the front of the carriage, the last compartment; swinging through the darkness that was only a prelude to the mysteries waiting beyond the final window.

He reached it in one last frantic scramble, hesitated a second, then squirmed inside, blundered to his feet in the dim yellow light, stood unsteadily on the swaying dirty floor.

And in the brief moment while he stood there, the invisible landscape outside thundering past, the interior of the compartment reflected weakly in the smeared window panes, the sooty wind churning at his back, he passed beyond certain boundaries, entered a world where actions were answered with rewards, where commitments were never betrayed, where it *was* possible to step twice into the same river.

And this time, there would be no errors, no hesitations.

For in the far corner, facing the engine, her blond head under the brown school hat bent over a book, sat Olwen.

Waiting.

He smiled as he moved towards her, no longer uncertain now, his fingers no longer clumsy. He knew, with a great surge of joy and triumph, that she had at last joined him, had moved with him from the dull daylight crudities to the warm yellow island of his nights.

Then the head turned slowly towards him, the blond hair brushing the shoulders; lifted, the wide hat-brim raising its curtain of shadow from the face.

But it was not the face of Olwen, warmed with welcome and desire, that smiled up at him; instead, stunned, he saw Nella's thin brown mask, the thin lips an obscene wound that bled sly mockery. Saw, recognized dimly, a parodied school uniform, an ill-fitting blond wig, accoutrements from a world of betrayal he had thought gone for ever.

He heard the thin shrillness of the engine's whistle as the train approached the Leith siding, felt the slowing drag of the reluctant wheels as the driver closed the regulator. His throat was very dry, and his fingers — suddenly clumsy again — ceased their movements. And he knew with dreadful certainty that one woman — and only one — had waited for him always, hiding cunningly within the other's promise; felt the skin begin to prickle at the back of his neck.

Then she smiled at him with sly dark malice; lit a cigarette a little clumsily, the match-flame jerking unevenly in the rocking compartment. Drew in a deep lungful of smoke, leaned towards him.

He watched his hands move, saw them reach her before the smoke rose to her pursed lips.

Later he sat huddled in the far corner of the compartment, his face pressed to the glass, evading the dull reflected images — the hateful uniform, the wide sensual face, the tangled crown of blond hair, the slumped and immobile figure. Locking his mind to the rattling of the wheels on the track, the high whistle at the signals, the rising crescendo of the pistons as the driver opened the regulator on the long straight by the river, he waited in craven silence for the slowing beat, for the panting shuffle as the train slowed at the edge of town, slid slowly towards the dim station. Waited for the moment when he would be able to escape at last from her unbearable silent contempt, rush off into the comforting night and the still and silent warmth of his narrow bed.

For nothing now was tolerable but loneliness, and he waited with desperate patience for the train to carry him to the last sanctuary.

Afternoon in Eldorado

Heat fused the pewter of the afternoon sky to the smoky line of the hills in a ragged weld, and along the tongue of the ridge curving down behind the house trees wavered drunkenly in the shimmering air.

Damn it, she thought, we're strangers here, as out of place as the bloody pot. She filled the bright aluminium saucepan from the bucket by the sink and set it on the blackened top of the old wood-stove. It gleamed there dully, its machined perfection quite alien to the old cottage. But no more alien, it seemed to her, than she was herself.

She stood, sweating gently, considering without humour the farcical necessity of a wood fire in the blistering tag-end of February. Then she turned away, lit a cigarette, abandoned the paradox of the pot and of her own situation. Sitting in a hard kitchen chair she stared through the window, past the skewed verandah posts and the gnarled and lichened skeletons of the apple trees, past the sagging wire fence, at the straight white ribbon of the deserted road.

Three degrees between the two of us, she thought, and we're living like peasants. Divorced from an ex-house filled with expensive and convenient gadgetry — for this, a wood fire for a cup of tea on a raging summer day. And a smelly dunny, showers from a five-gallon drum, dresses from the op shop.

Where the narrowing focus of the road disappeared into the cutting a mile away a tiny dot jiggled in the heat waves like some minute corpuscle flickering across the eye, too close to the retina for definition.

We have to *prove* things, she thought. Prove our rejection of the shoddy values, prove it by *action*. Live in a three-roomed shack in a town that no longer even exists. Get by on relief teaching and wallaby meat at twenty-five cents a pound. Embrace our self-imposed exile in a place no longer even mapped, where even the ghosts of the miners have long gone.

She stubbed out her cigarette.

The tiny dot in the distance was growing slowly, indecisively, in the uncertain air. Someone, someone walking? Who? From where? The Davidsons, two miles away? No, they had given up in the face of the long summer, retreated to their secret shame, the beach shack.

Who, then?

Someone, never mind.

Her eyes, half-blinded by the whiteness of the gravel road, faltered, her attention drifted to the trees that lined the path. Alan thought that the barren and long-untended orchard could be rejuvenated. Rework the trees, cut back hard at pruning time. He had read the books, knew the words. Pruning time was ... when? Autumn? Winter? She couldn't remember. Coolness, though, wind, rain, wood fires. Christ, wood fires ...

It was a man, she saw now, trudging steadily down the road, a black stick-figure against the blinding light. Towards Eldorado.

Eldorado.

They had found the old post-office sign and nailed it, a joke now long soured, on the door of the dunny. The dunny, a grey huddle of parched boards held together, she often thought, as much by habit as by the tired and rusty nails, the arthritic fingers of the old ivy stems.

It had all seemed so *right*. Selling up, moving. Five acres, an orchard, birds, space, a garden ...

Sorrel, twitch, onion-weed. And never enough water to spare to keep the straggling vegetables alive through the dry months.

A man, definitely a man. Tall, perhaps, thin. Impossible to tell with certainty in the wavering glare. A hump on his shoulder, a bundle of some kind ...

A sense of community, she thought: *that* was what we wanted. The land itself, and people, people who cared ...

But the people were so far away. Two miles to the Davidsons, more the other way to the Brents. The Brents. She liked Jenny. But Jenny ... Jenny seemed to *do* so little. Cook, wash, clean up, look after Terry and the kids. Not even a real garden after almost five years.

Would *she* end up like that? The thought frightened her. She had meant, really *meant*, to do so much: pottery, weaving, so much. But somehow things got in the way — the weedy garden with its choked soil, endless problems with the old stove, long trips for supplies, leaking tanks, washing up in a tiny plastic dish ... it all took so *long*.

Perhaps next year ...

In Jerusalem. She grimaced sourly, lit another cigarette. Behind her, on the stove, the water in the polished pot began to bubble gently.

Tea. Soon.

The man was closer now, his figure no longer distorted by the pulsing shimmers. Perhaps he'd stop, talk. She could offer him tea, the few scones remaining from yesterday's bout with the unpredictable oven.

My grandmother, she thought, she lived her whole bloody life in a world like this ...

And thinking of the old half-forgotten lady she was suddenly aware of an immense void in herself, an overwhelming lack. It wasn't that she felt less tough, less able, softer. But the *necessity* had departed. She and Alan were engaged in taming a wilderness that had been already once subdued, and abandoned. They were no more than children, the two of them, playing at being pioneers. If it all became too much for them they could run — there was always the old safe retreat; conformity, shelter in the last necessity. There was no belonging here for them because there was no true *need*, no desperation. Unlike real pioneers *they* could always go back. The truth was that they were as anomalous, as foreign, as the bright shoddy pot bubbling on the ancient stove.

She watched the man draw level with the gateway, pause in the middle of the road. Indisputably human, male, the sharp angularity of his figure framed by the gateposts, the crotchets of the twisted apple branches overhead. In sudden anguish that he might pass by, abandon her to the heat and despair of the day, she half rose in her chair, eyes fixed on him, willing him towards the shadows of the path.

Slowly, as if sensing her unvoiced invitation, he moved a few paces towards the gate. Paused again, looking up the dim tunnel of the path, his image sharp and clear. Tall, dark, dusty. A little older than she had thought ... forty, perhaps forty-five. Cheap dungarees — unworn, she noticed, at the work spots, cuffs and knees and thigh fronts. Shoes — not boots — cracked and crusted, down-at-heel. A dark-checked shirt, sleeves rolled to elbows, arms reddened, burnt but not yet tanned. Town, she thought, he's town, not country, even if he *has* got a short-back-and-sides, does carry a roped sugarbag on his back.

He stepped forward once again, this time less tentatively, moving with slow decision towards the gate. His face was lined, weathered more by years than wind and sun, and oddly light eyes lay deep in their sockets under the black bar of his eyebrows. His hair was dusted from the road.

She felt a sudden small flutter of something like panic.

And dismissed it quickly. Only his strangeness, his unexpected appearance in the day, had disturbed her for a moment. Looking for work, perhaps, escaping the queues and humiliations of the city. Tea, she thought, I'll lay on the old-fashioned country welcome …

His shoes crunched on the weedy gravel of the path as he moved through the sharp dappling of shadow.

The door was open, and she moved silently on bare feet towards it, losing sight of him for a moment.

When she stepped into the doorway he was already at the first rickety step at the bottom of the verandah, one foot raised to begin the small ascent. For a moment she felt the quick return of her momentary panic, something like a flush of fear as his shadow blocked out the light, washed all detail from his form. He seemed suddenly menacing, and she halted, flat-footed, as he mounted the two uneven steps, stood squarely, wordlessly, before her.

It will be all right, she thought, it's just the shadow, it'll pass. No harm, just the sudden surprise at the still flat blackness in the bright afternoon.

But as her eyes grew accustomed to the dimness of the verandah her apprehension did not lessen. Rather, it mounted, a tiny seed of panic germinating deep inside her, sending out tendrils of alarm as she watched his face reveal itself, developing slowly like the image on a photographic plate.

It was not the presence of any overt threat that alarmed her — for the narrow stubbled face, drifted with fine dust, was impassive, expressionless. The wide lips were slightly parted, relaxed, the grey eyes blank and empty.

She drew a deep breath, but found she could not speak. Instead, she took a single step backward, aware of her complete vulnerability, of the swing of her breasts beneath the looseness of her dress, of the dampness of thigh scissoring on thigh as she retreated.

And with her step backward, the stranger took one forward.

She opened her lips to break the sudden tautness in her throat. And heard only her ragged breathing, the soft shuffle of her feet moving backward across the bare floor.

Again he moved forward. Inside the doorway, he seemed to grow, to fill the small space completely.

Christ, she thought, Christ, it's just like the stories, he's going to *do* something to me …

Unspeakable images of violence crowded in on her, mixed with a sudden horror of losing consciousness, of being helpless, of not *knowing* what was happening … somehow that made it worse …

She could barely think, found herself already halfway across the room, backing away as quickly as he moved forward. His utter silence and impassivity menaced her far more than any shouted threats.

He knew, she thought, he knew I'd be alone; saw the smoke, no car, knew it, came down the path knowing …

She watched his eyes, tried to find some hint of weakness, of erosion of purpose. But there was nothing. A blankness, a cold greyness, widening black pupils that held firm in some unthinkable resolve.

At her back she felt the growing heat, and realized that she had retreated as far as the stove. In sudden fear she reached behind her with spread hands as if to ward off the new enemy, felt on her palms the dull beating heat from the black iron. And felt the fingers of her right hand close round the smooth moulded plastic of the pot handle.

Slowly, carefully, she raised the bubbling pot, the sound of its boiling suddenly loud in the silence, and moved it round her body, clasping the familiar handle with both hands. Her eyes never left his face, she dared not look down at the pot but she moved slightly, a tiny threatening gesture that slopped the scalding water, hinted at a full underarm swing that would drench him, burn, blind.

For a long moment they stood motionless in the hot silent room, locked a pace apart in the stasis of threat and counter-threat.

Then, unbelievingly, she found herself moving, taking a single hesitant step forward, towards him, towards the unchanged blankness of the unblinking eyes.

He moved. Shifted his weight slowly, took his own inevitable step backward from the menace of the pot.

Slowly, cautiously, hands tensed on the pot handle, eyes locked on his, she walked him back across the room. At the doorway he paused almost imperceptibly, and she made a bolder movement that spattered his dusty toecaps. He stepped back quickly, through the doorway, onto the verandah.

She stopped in the doorway, holding him with her eyes, and slowly moved her right hand from the pot handle, raised it above her head, slowly, slowly, felt the smooth stock of the shotgun on its nails above the architrave. Shifting her hand to the point of balance she lifted it down, swung it awkwardly into the crook of her arm. Wedging it there, she drew back both hammers, the skin of her thumb slippery on the worn metal. It was kept loaded, both barrels, against the occasional visits by tiger snakes to the damp coolness beneath the tankstand. Still crooking the gun she slipped her fingers into the guard, found the triggers, raised the barrels.

He continued to back away. He did not hurry. Once, halfway down the path, he stumbled a little on a loose stone, and she sensed the effort in him as he kept his eyes on hers, ignoring the uncertain footing. She stopped then, set down the pot carefully on the path, raised the gun in both hands.

Still he moved backward towards the gate, his eyes watching her coldly, blankly, over the twin shining barrels.

Once through the gate he moved quickly but smoothly, broke contact, stepped smartly out onto the road, turned his head and marched stiffly away, his worn heels kicking spurs of dust behind him.

She sagged against the gatepost, rested the fore-end of the gun on the grey timber, and found suddenly that she was shaking, that her jaw was trembling. But she did not move until he was half a mile away, his shape dissolving again in the dancing air.

When she was certain that he was gone she carefully eased down the hammers, moved back into a patch of shade, pressed her damp back against the crusted bark of a tree. The afternoon woke about her in a drowning hum of insects. She had the feeling of returning after a long journey.

That's it, she thought. The end. We're packing it in, whatever Alan says. Christ, I could have *killed* him ...

And she felt the beginnings of tears prickle behind her eyes, a hard constriction grow in her throat. And readied herself for the luxury of total collapse.

Then she remembered Jenny.

The man was headed east. The road would take him past the Brents. Terry and the boys were off in the orchards of the river valley, and Jenny would be alone.

She ran up the path to the verandah, past the shiny cooling pot, stopped for a moment to tug on her old work boots, then trotted round the side of the house, past the tankstand, through the dying vegetable garden. It was three miles by the road, but only a mile and a half the back way, along the creek bed, up the old woodchip track and over the ridge.

On the rutted crumbling path by the dry creek she lengthened her stride, her boots crackling in the short straw-dry grass, the metal of the gun barrels clamped to her chest. She had forgotten her hat, and the heat struck her like the ring of an axe. Sweat stung her eyes and the loose boots chafed at her heels. Thudding up the track towards the distant ridge, her breath sobbing in her ears, her thigh muscles trembling and faltering, she felt a strangeness begin inside her. It grew a little with each hard-fought stride, a fierce passion as deep and sudden as it was unfamiliar: a passion that embraced her own sweating body, the inflexible earth, the heat, the loneliness, the woodstove, the smelly dunny, all of it. As she staggered onto the crown of the ridge a breath of wind, hot but fresh, touched her face, and she knew that for the first time she was close to some kind of truth: that there *was* some meaning, that it was never merely a matter of passivity, of survival, or even of taming. It was much more, she knew now.

With a fierce surge of pride she pounded down the gentle slope towards the valley, the lethal metal hugged to her body, and swung into the shadowed tunnel of the track. It was more than just coming back — it was *claiming.*

Shit, she thought, her feet flying over the ruts, just watch me go, grandma, just you watch me go ...

In the Money

'How much longer?' asked the small man. 'We've been in this frigging hole for three weeks already.'

'Soon,' said the big man.

They stood together in the slant of yellow light that spilled from the open doorway of the big galvanized-iron canteen. The night air was warm and heavy.

'But when?' said the small man.

'Next pay-day.'

'Christ, that's nearly a fortnight away ...'

'Don't worry, Jimmy,' said the big man. 'We'll be gone before the wet starts.'

'I hope so,' said Jimmy. 'This bloody mine's giving me the creeps.' He paused. 'Who is it, anyway, Vic? Have you picked him out yet?'

'Yeah — the big Dutchman.'

'What, the big dark one in the Alimak crew?'

'That's him.'

'Oh.' Jimmy seemed to lose interest.

'Come on,' said Vic. 'Let's get back to the donga, get an early night.'

'You're like a bloody old woman ...'

'Never mind,' said the big man. And he nudged Jimmy gently before him down the stony track that led through thick darkness to the flat behind the sprawling mess hut where the grubby dongas were ranked like abandoned trams. At the bottom of the hill they passed through the pool of dusty light under the lone lamp outside the tiny post office. The small man hummed to himself, shuffled his feet in the fine red earth, sniffed at the air as he swung his head from side to side. His fine blond hair was sweat-plastered against his bony skull. The big man slouched behind him. The light caught the ridges of scar tissue round his eyes, his knobbed and broken knuckles, and the wires of silver in his thick dark hair.

Then they moved out of the light, dim shadows again in the darkness, moving silently towards the dongas.

'It's Saturday, isn't it?' said Jimmy, pushing his greasy plate away. The breakfast crowd in the mess hut was thinning. 'What we gonna do?'

'Have a bludge this morning,' said Vic, between bites of cold fried egg. 'Do some roadwork this arvo ...'

Jimmy pushed back his chair in sudden disgust, stood up, and walked away towards the door.

The big man took no notice. Sweat was trickling gently down his face, coalescing into tiny runnels that coursed slowly over his pitted honey-brown skin. He finished his meal, drank the last of his tea, stood up, belched, walked outside.

Jimmy was waiting for him, sitting surly on the step in the hard sunlight. He stood up wordlessly, and they walked away together.

Vic sat on a rock in the sparse shade of a bottle tree, his eyes slitted against the blue glare of the lake. He could see Jimmy's distant figure shimmering and bobbing in the heat haze of the long shore. He looked down, away from the heat of the light; rolled a cigarette, sat watching the tiny ta-ta lizards scurrying through the yellow rocks.

Jimmy's rasping breath was louder than his footfalls. His shorts clung to his muscular thighs, his sweater was dark with moisture, his face congested with heat and effort. When he reached the rock he flung himself down, and lay with his head half-buried in a clump of cape gooseberry.

When his breathing had slowed a little, he said, 'It's too … too bloody hot … for this …' He struggled to sit up, pulled off his sweater, slung it across Vic's lap. 'Smell that…'

The big man raised it to his nostrils.

'I'm not sweating bloody sweat,' said Jimmy, 'I'm sweating bloody *ammonia* …'

Vic opened the old haversack at his feet, pulled out a can of soft drink, passed it to Jimmy. From his pocket he took a small jar, shook out a handful of white salt tablets. 'Take these,' he said. 'Otherwise you'll get cramps.'

Jimmy swallowed the tablets, drained the lukewarm can. 'No more of this,' he said. 'I can't take it. Anyway, I'm fit enough …'

'You're never fit enough. Besides, the Dutchman's fit, too.'

'I can take him.'

'You sure?'

Jimmy was silent for a moment. 'I won't go back inside that place again,' he said. 'You know that, don't you?'

'I know it, mate.'

'I can take the Dutchman. I can take ten frigging Dutchmen, before breakfast …'

'Sure you can.'

'Remember that time in the Manly cells? How it took six of them to keep me down?' And he laughed, his face suddenly childlike and happy. 'I just kept gettin' up, didn't I?'

'That's all you've got to do, Jimmy …'

And Jimmy lay back, his head buried in the soft, fragrant leaves.

In a little while he stood up, and they began the long walk back through the spinifex to the camp.

'Now?' said Jimmy.

Vic nodded.

The mess hall was crowded, but the evening meal was drawing to a close, and there was a small crush around the tea urn. Jimmy had filled his cup, begun to turn towards his table. Then he brushed against the man, jogging his arm, spilling hot tea over the man's legs and belly.

'Hey! Look what you're bloody doing!' He was big, dark, and heavily muscled, with shoulder-length hair pulled back under a red headband.

Jimmy looked up at him. 'Stupid friggin' squarehead … want to look what you're doin' …' And then, before the Dutchman could speak again, move, Jimmy hit him twice, a quick, stinging left-right, and the man was stumbling back with blood pouring from his nose. He ran his hand down his face, looked at the blood, and began to move towards Jimmy.

Vic was already moving in, a long punch away from the Dutchman. But the mess manager, a pale heavyweight in sweated white ducks, was between them, swinging an axe-handle.

'You two want to fight, you fight outside …'

Jimmy was laughing, watching the Dutchman.

'Come on,' said the Dutchman. 'You want it so bad, let's go outside.'

'Anytime,' said Jimmy, laughing, shuffling his feet, loosening his shoulders.

'Outside, all of you …' said the mess manager.

Then the Dutchman, looking at Jimmy, began to smile. 'You little runt,' he said. 'I *ought* to bloody hammer you …'

'You couldn't hammer a bloody tack,' said Jimmy. 'You're just like all squareheads, all wind and piss.'

The Dutchman lost his smile. 'You'd last about two seconds, you skinny little fart!'

Jimmy was suddenly very still. When he spoke, his voice

was cold. 'I've got a thousand bucks says I can last longer than you, squarehead.'

Even the mess manager was silent.

Then Vic spoke. 'I've got another thousand says the same. How about it?' He looked at the mess manager. 'You hold the stakes?'

The mess manager nodded slowly.

'Pay night?' said Vic, looking at the Dutchman.

Jimmy ripped open his shirt and began to unbuckle a money-belt.

'Well?' said Vic.

The Dutchman nodded slowly, not taking his eyes from Jimmy. 'All right.' Then he turned his head to look at Vic for the first time, and there was a faint haze of puzzlement and uncertainty in his brown eyes.

Jimmy lay on his bed, eyes closed.

'It's a pity we had to lay out so much at evens,' said Vic. 'But I'll get the rest covered at odds.'

Jimmy opened his eyes. 'How much altogether?'

'Two thousand from the Dutchman and his mates … another two gees at maybe fours, fives … who knows? … I reckon maybe twelve gees altogether, plus our stake.'

'Then we can go?' said Jimmy. 'Can we, Vic? Somewhere where it's quiet … and cool?'

'Sure, mate. We'll beat the wet, run south.' Then, 'Listen, Jimmy — you sure you can take him?'

Jimmy closed his eyes again. 'Don't worry about it.'

After a while Vic lay down too, and the silence closed over the small hot room.

The crowd of several hundred had already gathered under the lights on the square of starved grass by the big movie screen. Lightning flickered low on the northern horizon.

They came quietly out of the darkness, the two of them, moved slowly through the crush to the place where the

Dutchman was waiting for them. He wore shorts and a singlet, and looked very big and solid. Jimmy, in his old jeans and white shirt, seemed thin and under-nourished.

'You both ready?' asked the mess manager, who was also referee.

'Ready,' said the Dutchman.

Jimmy nodded silently, and peeled off his shirt.

'Right,' said the mess manager. 'You both know the rules … no rounds, no spells, and she's over when one of you can't get up.' He waved his axe-handle. 'You set, then?'

They both nodded.

'Then fight!'

A sudden silence fell over the crowd. There was no sound except for the soft slither of feet on the dusty grass.

And then, suddenly, Jimmy moved, so fast that he seemed to dissolve into a blur of flesh. He struck the other man twice in the belly, hard, jabbing blows. Then, as the Dutchman's hands came down, he punched for the head — left, right, left again — and then he was away, as quickly as he had come. There was blood on the Dutchman's face. He fell back a moment, then came forward cautiously.

Jimmy waited. And when the Dutchman was close, dropped his guard a little, rode the punch when it came, slipped inside it, hammered two swift punches to the belly, then two long lefts that opened up a cut over the Dutchman's eye. But as he moved away, the Dutchman caught him on the head with a solid right, and he stumbled a moment. Then he was away again, dancing and weaving easily.

And so it went for several minutes. Jimmy would slide in, land a punch or two, take one, slip away. He seemed still to be breathing easily, while the Dutchman's chest was heaving.

Then the Dutchman swung a little wildly as Jimmy moved in, caught him squarely in the ribs, and Jimmy grunted and clinched. He clung for a long moment, his chin buried, hammering. Then he broke away, swinging one last punch at the Dutchman's cut eye.

But it seemed now that Jimmy was tiring. He seemed a little slower, and he grimaced when the heavy blows struck him. The big man's animal strength seemed to be carrying him beyond the power of Jimmy's punches, and for perhaps ten minutes Jimmy took more and more of the heavy punches, his light frame jolting with the force of the bare-knuckle blows. His right ear was swelling badly, and his lip was gashed. Blood masked both men's faces, and their skins were mottled with knuckled roses.

Suddenly Jimmy was down. The Dutchman rushed in, but Jimmy was up and gone. As the big man turned, Jimmy planted himself firmly, threw a long looping right to the forehead that checked the other man; a left jab flicked blood from his cut eye, and a right looped up below the hollow of his jaw.

The Dutchman stood flatfooted, seemed for a moment about to collapse. Then he lunged, swinging. Two great blows struck Jimmy, lifted him almost from his feet, and the Dutchman was hammering, beating him down by pure weight and fury. Jimmy's face was very white under the blood. His lip was badly split, and his nose was broken. His hands hung low, and his shoulders sagged. It seemed that only the strength of his sinewy legs kept him from falling.

The Dutchman paused, moved in carefully. He swung once, and Jimmy caught the punch on his arm, rode inside it.

And then a mad kind of magic seemed to take Jimmy. He ceased even to guard himself. His hands dropped, his feet moved squarer, and he lowered his chin. He moved in slowly, muffling the Dutchman's next punch, and struck him twice below the sternum, punches that seemed to crackle with electricity. And the power seemed to drain from the Dutchman's thick body. Jimmy rose a little on the balls of his feet, dropped his right shoulder; he hit the Dutchman once under the ear with his right, and the Dutchman's legs buckled a little; he struck again in the same place, and paused as the man began to stagger; and then he followed him, and, beating down the protecting hands, he struck again, and again, and again. The first punch broke the man's jaw; the second — a short upward thrust with the heel of his hand — caught the nose and forced the head back; and the third, a long wicked hook, took the Dutchman in the throat.

Jimmy stood back then, trembling and wavering, and smiling a nightmare smile, as he watched the Dutchman fall to his knees, moaning and gulping for breath. He waited for the man to collapse, to fall. But he did not, he stayed on his knees, groaning, blinded by blood, trying to clamber back to his feet.

The mess manager began to move forward, but Vic touched his arm, shook his head, and he stopped.

And gently, almost reverently, as an executioner might, Jimmy stepped forward, measured, and swung once, hard and short, to the spot below the Dutchman's ear. And the big man toppled at last, lay still on the dusty trampled grass.

A great cumulative sigh seemed to rise from the crowd. Vic ran forward. But he stopped a pace short of Jimmy, who stood pale and bloody, trembling a little. 'You all right?' he asked.

Jimmy nodded. 'Just don't touch me for a while ...'

'I know ...' Vic turned to the mess manager. 'Fair fight?'

'Fair fight,' said the mess manager, and began counting out money.

People were picking up the Dutchman and carrying him away.

'Come on,' said Vic. He hung the white shirt over Jimmy's shoulders. It was bloodied in a moment. Then he followed as Jimmy walked steadily and delicately out through the silent crowd. And, a hundred paces down the track, beyond the final tell-tale light, caught him as he fell, carried him carefully and gently back to the donga.

The air inside the closed donga was hot and stale. Jimmy lay supine in his bed. Vic knelt beside him. He worked for a long time. First he sponged away the blood and sweat, and washed the bruised face. With an awkward arm round Jimmy's shoulders, he lifted him, taped his chest with a wide strip of plaster. Then he cleaned the knuckles and swabbed them with mercurochrome, and taped them too. With a needle and fine surgical thread he carefully stitched the cut eye. He paused then for a moment, rocking back on his stiff knees. He said, 'You awake?'

'Yeah …' Jimmy's voice was hoarse and nasal, and he seemed to have difficulty moving his puffed lips.

'I'm just about finished,' said Vic. 'You want a drink?'

'Yeah.' Jimmy did not open his eyes.

Vic reached behind him, lifted the tumbler to Jimmy's lips. Jimmy sipped a little, lay back. 'How am I?' he said.

'Not too bad. A couple of ribs cracked, your nose gone again, a cut eye, a couple of teeth …'

'Knuckle's broke, too,' said Jimmy. 'I felt it go at the end there …'

'I know,' said Vic. 'Don't worry about it.'

'No.'

Then, 'He took some stopping, didn't he?'

'He sure did.'

'But I wrapped him up, didn't I?'

'You bet.'

'How much we get?'

'Nearly fifteen thousand, all told.'

Jimmy opened his eyes for a moment. 'When can we get out of here?'

'As soon as you can travel.'

'Tomorrow, then …'

Then, 'Vic? Where we gonna go?'

'Wherever you want to go, mate.'

'Somewhere where it's cool and quiet ...'

'Yeah.'

'You know somewhere like that?'

'We'll find somewhere ...' And he got to his feet, a big hard man, past his prime, in grimy singlet and underpants; stood there looking down at the thin battered body under the single sheet, at the beaten puffy face.

Jimmy opened his eyes once more. 'You finished now?'

'Yeah.'

Jimmy closed his eyes again. 'What you waitin' for, then? Get into bed ...'

Vic stood silent for a moment. Then he switched off the light, lifted the sheet, climbed in beside Jimmy. Cramped in the narrow bed, he lay beside the thin body, listening to the harsh nasal breathing. Slowly it took on the slow rhythm of sleep. But he lay awake for a long time, sweating in the hot night, listening to Jimmy's breathing, staring into the thick darkness.

The Sadist

It is a Tuesday afternoon, and the first truly warm day of spring. Warm enough, almost, for shirt-sleeves, for the first cautious exposure of winter-blanched flesh. Tuesday, Maisie's day. He waits for her in his large bare house behind the sprawl of the hospital. A dying residential area, said the mayor, opening a new Coles warehouse three blocks away. But it is not true. A quiet ghetto, perhaps, but alive and persistent. For ten years he has lived there in his sixty-year-old white weatherboard house. And has spoken three times to his neighbour on the left, never to the one on the right, round the corner in Eglington Street.

Maisie. A soft name. It brings him visions of green oats, of summer, of corn with long silk tassels. She is large, soft, generous. Blonde, full-breasted ... buxom. Buxom — the word has always delighted him. There are no Maisies in the jeans of the new generation.

So he waits, not quite patiently.

The truth is, the season's unease lies under his breast-bone a little cankerously.

Spring is difficult. It has always been difficult for him. Oftener than beginnings, it seems to bring endings. And from September on, he is inclined to feel a certain unfocused malaise. By December, late November even, the worst is past, and by late summer he is on an even keel again. March, he has found, is a good time for beginnings.

He met Maisie in March, a little over six months ago.

But the real beginning had been even earlier than that.

It took him some time to frame the advertisement. A matter of revision, consideration, review. In his mind, before ever pen was set to paper. It was a kind of rebellion in the end, and he had the grace to see that it must be presented with some style. This city is the problem. This small city. It is too large for the friendly tolerance of a country town, where minor eccentricities are recognized, accepted, submerged in a kind of familial tolerance. And too small for the anonymity of a real city. Besides, its ingrown conservatism is of a vicious and unforgiving nature. He sees the city's soul in the image of a rat cowering behind a cash register. Some discretion would be necessary, he knew, if he were to avoid unpleasantness. But above all, polish. And style.

The advertisement was, as well as a small rebellion, a last resort. He had watched — for months, a year — the columns of a certain national weekly. But in vain — he saw never a single call from this city. There were occasional entries, certainly ... studs, would-be swingers, half-hearted queers ... but nothing that promised resolution for his own stern exigencies. So, with the spring behind him, he made his decision, took paper and pen, and threw himself on the distant mercy of the newsprint.

He spent much time on the draft. Dignity was essential, and he strove hard to exclude any hint of coarseness, of vulgarity.

LAUNCESTON, he began. Plain enough. And there would be guessing games, he thought, and a spiteful secret canvassing of friends.

A description. FORMER SCHOOLMASTER. A nice touch. A respected profession, with hints of sternness, asceticism, erudition. Reassuring. He saw no point in dwelling on the brevity of his association with the profession; had his legacy not intervened he might even have been permitted to persist.

SINGLE. Truth, truth, and comfortable connotations of a bachelor lifestyle. No complications. Indeed, he wished — sometimes a little desperately — for a minor complication or two. EARLY FORTIES. There he deviated, in vanity, a little from the strict truth. But only a little.

And now the message, the kernel. He had stalked it carefully through the underbrush of the preliminaries, and its shape was clear. He defined it firmly. WILL ENROL LADY, ANY AGE, FOR PRIVATE TUITION AND STRICT OLD-FASHIONED DISCIPLINE. It was no time for counting words or dollars, and he toyed for a little with the idea of RUBENS TYPE PREFERRED; but in the end struck it out — it lacked delicacy, hinting of blowsy barmaids. ENROL — he liked that touch particularly. Enrol, enrol … a course of study, a programme of learning, admission, tuition, schooling, study, supervision … and discipline. *Discipline.* Enough said.

I AM A FIRM BUT UNDERSTANDING TEACHER. A clarion. Declarative, but not bold. Confident, though, and unequivocal.

He made a final fair copy, admired it a little, and sealed the envelope, worrying only a little at possible breaches of the promised anonymity. He had acquaintances, neighbours, after all. And this town … this town …

But he set his doubts aside — with discipline — and his step was firm enough as he walked down the hill to the mail box.

His advertisement appeared. Once, twice, a third time. He waited.

Two weeks after the last appearance he began to despair. Thought of moving to a large city where commerce might be expected to cater to his needs. Considered sedatives. Drank neat whisky for the first time in years. Fondled the outsize dog-collar, the knouts and straps. Masturbated sadly. Filled his evenings with twice and thrice seen movies — until the usherettes turned their contempt and suspicion on him. Sleep became a solace, a drug, and for hours in the long mornings he hung at its edges, struggling out at last only to watch, from the blind's edge, the postman pass him by.

Then, one morning, when hope was almost totally eroded, he found shuffled in a small handful of bills, circulars and receipts, a large plain envelope. And inside it, another envelope — small, white, Woolworths self-seal. Sniffed it. Held it to the light. Felt something stiff inside. He laid it carefully aside, unopened, on the kitchen table. With nervousness dry at the top of his throat, and anticipation almost unendurable, he boiled the jug and made coffee. Lit a cigarette. Sat for a moment or two gazing blankly out the window at the imitation grey brick of his neighbour's wall. And at last took out a steak-knife and slit the crisp paper of the envelope.

A photograph!

It amazed him that a stranger should so display herself — to another stranger — display all that blank receptivity, that willingness to realize possibilities. But even in his shock at the naked boldness of it, he realized that it savoured of some deep need for his ministrations.

He began to construct her from the flat glossy card. Blonde. A little faded. Fortyish, perhaps? Pale, solid, a little over-blown. And a certain regretful sadness seemed to linger at the monochrome mouth. A wistfulness. She was … working class, he thought. And was surprised. But bourgeois matrons would be perhaps too engrossed in bowling and bulbs; and although he had expected a certain sophistication, it was plainly lacking. Yet an appeal edged at him; inferiority, knowledge, admission of it, lay implicit in the mute offering.

At last he unfolded the brief note. Thin, lined paper. From a pad. He suspected Woolworths again. The cover would have a bluebird, a Royal, or perhaps Clark Gable. The writing was large, rounded (as was she), childish. He looked back at the picture, finding now a hint of the girl herself in the uncertain melancholy of the face.

And came at last to consider the text.

'Dear Sir,' she began, 'I am writing in response to your advertisement. I am interested in the tuition you mention, and would like further details of the course of study.'

He wondered if a certain irony might not lie behind the words; but the simplicity of the handwriting belied the possibility. 'I feel my life is lacking,' she wrote, 'in guidance, and would welcome a firm hand. Perhaps we could meet to discuss the matter.' (He noted for the first time the lack of address on the letter. It seemed that she was not yet ready to risk *everything*, to sacrifice *every* privacy. The realization disappointed him a little, but he curbed his impatience.) 'I will wait in the Mall at eleven o'clock next Tuesday morning. Please wear a white shirt and carry a book. You will know me from the photo. Yours sincerely, Maisie W.'

How did she guess, in this age of peacockery, that he wore, habitually, white shirts? He wondered, feeling a slight twinge, if his advertisement had not been a little *too* revealing.

And she was far from illiterate. Crisp and to the point. Preliminary understanding might be accomplished without too great a difficulty.

And so he came to the Mall on a hot March morning when the leaves on the captive trees hung limply, awaiting autumn; when brown edges showed on the parched azaleas, and the heat rose from the tiles and mixed with the tinny outpourings of the loudspeakers. He was early, and strolled for a while — hiding his nervousness — among the morning shoppers. He suspected that he was watched … from Fitzgeralds, perhaps, from Coles, or from the wide aisles of the book shop. He settled at last by the tourist-department dog-box, puffing spuriously on an unfamiliar pipe.

Nothing.

But as the post-office clock struck the hour, she came to him. Not from the shops, but from the bank at the far end of the pedestrian walk. Cunning. He wondered how long she had waited inside the cool polished hall, how many deposit slips had been defaced and discarded.

She wore white — not virginal, but sacrificial — and walked straight towards him. He flicked a quick glance at his own image in a cluttered window, then turned to accept her.

Deferring the promise of her body, he looked carefully at her face; at the wide blue eyes, the slight fullness below the chin, the faint hint of lines at mouth and eye-corner, the gentle droop of lips. Still untanned and pale, she had evaded summer. A pearling of perspiration glowed high on her forehead about the fine hair roots. He felt a rising triumph at her vulnerability, at the animal scent of uncertainty that rose from her flesh.

Took her arm, just above the elbow, firm finger probing gently.

'Have you been waiting long?' Her voice was strangely light for so full-bodied a woman. He smiled, shaking his head a little, sensing some cautious mockery behind the words.

He led her towards Charles Street, still holding her arm, and she seemed content to walk beside him, matching his silence. In the park he found a vacant seat beneath the heavy green canopy of oak leaves. Sunlight struck boldly at the fountain in its lake of dusty asphalt, children leaned above the scummed water barracking goldfish.

He turned to her, smiling, feeling still that no words were necessary. In the deep shade, her skin finding new undertones of violet light, her need seemed plain enough.

But he spoke all the same, laughing silently behind his face.

But seriousness overtook him later, and a certain solemnity overlaid his triumph. A gentle beginning, he had decided long ago. No rushing. So he took her gently through the prelude to winter.

The only bare boards in his house lay in the front hall, and it was there, capsuled together in the dimness, that he made her kneel, head bent, eyes downcast, while he stood above her and read for nearly thirty minutes from Trollope. In the beginning she shuffled uneasily, as the edges of the hard boards bit into her soft knees. But he frowned, marking his place with a patient finger, until she was still again, subdued and properly contrite. At the end of the reading he bent and slapped her lightly on the buttocks, aroused suddenly at the touch of soft uncorseted flesh shuddering a little under his fingers. Then raised her gently, compassionately, and waited while she massaged her red kneecaps. Her smile was grateful and a little timid, now.

He led her to the living room, guided her to a chair, poured white wine.

She explained nothing to him, ever, of her life. But he learned, as the weeks passed, of her widowhood, of her two teenaged daughters, of her just-sufficient income. It seemed to him that she lived — for six days each week — a life indistinguishable from that of any other suburban widow. He believed that she had no lovers, perhaps even no friends. Yet she seemed to recognize no emptiness, beyond the need that lay at the root of her visits each Tuesday afternoon. He never pressed her, felt no need to fill in the blanks; took indeed a curious pleasure at the lack of resolution in his view of her. She existed on Tuesdays, and that was sufficient. A little poignant, even. For her part, she showed no more inclination than did he to extend the ambit of their relationship beyond the Tuesday hours. But she never missed a week, was never late.

He guided her slowly, savouring the gradual focusing of her desire, watching its intensity mount towards his own. But he was restrained, patient, never pushed too hard. It was not until the fifth week that he introduced the riding-crop, let it bite a little at the soft whiteness of her back, naked for the first time. She cried a little, then, and the tears of pain struck deliciously at him. No pleasure, no violence, was complete without that twinge of compassion. It was not merely a sauce, a sharpness, but a necessary condition of his mounting greed for her. That day, on leaving, she kissed his hand.

On her next visit he made her strip in the cold bedroom — it was April now — and walked around her, marvelling at the sudden modesty, the profusion of unpunished flesh, the ache of happy humilation in her eyes. He bound her lightly, and knouted her a little. His joy, he felt, was approaching some climax.

It came the next week. Prudent of his own expected nakedness, he had heated the bedroom for some hours. Into its warmth he brought her, stripped her, spread-eagled her face down on the great old bed, bound hands and feet to the corners; and at last brought forth the dog-collar and tightened it about her trembling neck. He found that his breathing was a little ragged as he watched the round mountains of her buttocks, faintly aquiver. And reached for the new ivory-handled whip.

Later he found that he could recapture, in almost unbelieving detail, the final triumph of the day; could see, as from some external vantage point — the wardrobe's top perhaps — the absurd and glorious tableau of his wild ascendancy.

Astride her, knees deep in eiderdown, he impaled and rode her, the red weals on her white back bars of hot joy across his vision, her buttock-twitches gripping him, mastery thundering at last in his ears.

She cried again, later, in joy. And he melted a little at her vulnerability.

But as he sat alone at his fire that night, the rain rattling at the ancient iron on his roof, a certain sadness overtook him. And he had a sense of some final arrival.

So now it is Tuesday again, and in the nervous spring he waits for her, aware that his uneasiness is something more than seasonal. For some time now he has been aware of some lack, some flatness in his responses. Oh, they have come far now, he and Maisie, far from the naive experiments of those early days; the afternoons are filled with subtleties, with small perversions so neat, with responses so trained and calculated, that their pleasure is prolonged at will. There is less overt damage too, more excruciating pains and joys to be secured by small twists of new knowledge. Fear, too; he is aware of growing fear in her, and of its ready acceptance. And he still thrills a little to it, and offers reassurance only at the very limits of tolerance. He feels a growing respect in her, and an abasement that is not far short of absolute.

But ... but ...

But.

Something in her ... fails to echo now ...

He knows that she will come soon. From his bedroom window he watches the steepness of the street beyond the bare hydrangea stems with their pregnant buds. And he is dimly conscious that the dictates of the treacherous season must be accommodated. But how?

Born on the west wind, she enters the street a block away, fullness on fullness, acquiescence implicit in her firm bare calves, her swooping hips.

He knows that she is watching, already, for his appearance; senses the small thrills already tingling in her. And feels a sudden weight descending tiredly upon him.

Before she reaches the narrow gate, he has withdrawn. The door is locked, the blinds closed, the house silent behind its claws of unpruned hydrangea. He lies upon the bed, alone, quite still, while her footsteps wander about the garden, from door to door and back again; while her empty knocking haunts the tall spaces of his life. And he does not stir.

At last he hears the faltering footsteps, slow in puzzlement and disappointment, receding down the cracked asphalt, drawing away, fading in the gusts of wind.

He closes his eyes, finally, knowing that he has answered the spring's difficulty, the endings implicit in his own seasons. He has said goodbye to it all — for now: bidden her a silent goodbye, too. And knows the reason. For somewhere in his warm pink winter afternoons, something has retreated from him, fled quietly.

For he no longer pities her, he finds.

And must wait again for spring to pass.

Nails of Love,
Nails of Death

He was hunkered down beside the newly turned earth of the garden bed when the battered old VW swung in through the narrow gate and slid to a skewed stop at the head of the steps. He paused, watching, as the driver's door opened and the girl got out. For a moment she stood, her body hidden from him by the dented red body of the car, an arm laid on the rusty curve of the roof, looking out over the sprawl of the city, the distant windings of the river. The light wind stirred her lank black hair, and she lifted one pale hand to brush a long strand from her eyes.

When she moved he lost sight of her for a moment as she passed behind the car. Then she reappeared at the top of the steps, started down. She stooped a little to avoid the low branches of the apple tree, and he realized that she was nearly as tall as he was. But much thinner.

She stopped beside him on the narrow concrete path, a plastic carry-bag in each hand. The sleeves of her grey cardigan reached almost to her knuckles, and pale-pink apple petals were caught in her hair, hair as black as his own. But she was pale, the skin of her face almost translucent. He felt, in his stocky tanned body, suddenly thick and clumsy. Her eyes were a deep and sleepy blue.

'Hullo,' she said, standing flat-footed in her cheap thongs, the breeze pressing the thin folds of the long green dress against the backs of her thighs. Fine wisps of hair drifted about her face; a face pale, high-cheek-boned, a little too square.

'Hullo,' he said, watching the wide vulnerable mouth.

'I'm looking for number three,' she said, her voice low, as tenuous and insubstantial as the wind.

He stood up, flexed his knees, jerked his head towards the corner. 'Just round there.'

She nodded, moved away, drifted round the end of the building.

Number three was the lowest, the deepest, of the twelve flats, tucked away at the bottom level of the square three-storey block. It had been empty for nearly a month. No one stayed there long — it was too dark, too airless, too cold; its windows caught little sunlight, even in summer.

He went back to his planting.

Within a few minutes she was back. He heard her foot-steps, heard them pause, sensed her waiting, immobile, behind him. He glanced over his shoulder. The eyes, he saw, were really less sleepy than vacant. No, not that, either; but engaged, their vision turned inward, closed and private.

He raised his eyebrows at her.

'I've got some stuff in the car,' she said. 'Do you think you could give me a hand?'

'Sure.' He got to his feet, followed her up the steps to the car-park, brushing aside the new leaves bursting from the rough knots of the grapevine, dodging under the overhang of the apple tree.

The car was crammed with cardboard cartons, paper parcels, plastic bags. He began to unload, carrying them down to the flat. There was less than he had thought, and it took only a few minutes. Inside the dim flat her few pos-sessions seemed lost, swallowed up in the small cramped emptiness: a stack of records, a player, stained books, unpressed clothes, a few groceries.

He stood for a moment in the dim mustiness of the passage.

'Anything else? Can I help with anything?'

She stood in the doorway of the tiny kitchen. A little bright afternoon sunshine, filtered through the leaves of the peach tree, found its way into the room; against the vibrant green of the light her body, shadowed, took on a two-dimensional aspect, flat, anonymous.

She shook her head. 'No thanks.' Then, 'You're not Australian, are you?'

He smiled a little, almost shyly. 'No, Spanish. My name's Carlo.'

'Mine's Helen.'

'Well …'

'Thanks …'

He left her, still standing in the doorway, returned stolidly to his flowerbeds.

She came out again a little later, when the sun was edging down towards the distant sawtooth hills, sat on the low concrete wall watching him, smoking a cigarette in sharp quick puffs. He looked at her once, briefly, noting again the paleness, the translucency of her skin, the angular slightness of the body. She wasn't pretty, he decided, wouldn't be even if she were less thin. But there was an openness about her face, an innocent quality that made him think of the faces of young children; an openness denied by the veiled barrier of her eyes.

'You speak good English,' she said. 'Was it hard to learn?'

He laughed. 'No,' he said. 'I've been out here since I was a kid. We speak Spanish at home, but …' He shrugged.

'What are those?' She nodded at the plants in the bed, arranged in their neat rows like some small orderly army of grey-green spiders. 'I don't know anything about gardening. What sort are they?'

'Carnations,' he said.

'Oh.'

She seemed almost indifferent, as if her interest was a kind of obligation. She took a quick puff at her cigarette. 'What do you call them in Spanish?'

'*Clavel*,' he said, '*los claveles*.' He grinned at her, white teeth sudden against his dark unhandsome face. '*Clavos de amor, clavos de muerte*.'

With some effort she summoned another question. 'What's that? What's it mean?'

He laughed, turning to face her, squatting on his heels. 'It's a kind of play on words,' he said. '*Clavel* is a carnation, *clavelon* is a marigold. *Clavo* is a nail ... so, '*clavos de amor, clavos de muerte*' ... nails of love, nails of death ... carnations, marigolds ...'

Her eyes seemed to wake a little in genuine puzzlement. 'Why? What does it mean?'

'I don't know,' he said apologetically. 'Just a saying, you know, maybe nothing ...'

'Oh.'

'Just a saying ...'

She shivered. 'I'd better go in.'

He looked up at the sun, down at the shadows. 'Yeah,' he said. 'Nearly time to knock off.' He picked up the hose, turned the tap, and began to spray the small plants lightly. 'See you next week, maybe.'

'You come once a week, do you? Every week?'

He nodded. 'That's me, regular rounds. Here Tuesdays, over at Norwood Wednesdays, all over the place the rest of the week.' He smiled. 'If you want a hand any time ... you know ... odd jobs ... just give us a shout. The landlord doesn't mind.'

'Oh ... thanks.' Then she was gone, and the sun dipped below the top of the big quince tree at the bottom of the garden. Carlo began to gather his tools, load them into his old utility.

He didn't see her when he came to work the next week, although the shabby VW still stood crookedly in the car-park. Through the day he worked methodically, planting, weeding, watering, mowing; passing and repassing her green-painted door. But it remained closed, the opaque glass panel dark and blank.

'She's a quiet one,' said Mrs Sykes from number two, bringing out her garbage in the late afternoon. 'Hardly ever see hide nor hair ...'

'Doesn't she go to work?' asked Carlo.

Mrs Sykes shrugged, the pale bee-sting of her mouth indifferent in her puffy middle-aged face. Wriggling a finger under the towelling turban she scratched her scalp. 'Never seen her.' She stalked back towards her door. 'I think she's been sick ...'

Carlo began to trim the edges of the lawn with sharp precise strokes.

On the next Tuesday he had been working for several hours, repairing the grape trellis, training the passionfruit vine along the fence, when he heard her voice calling to him from the doorway.

'Would you like a cup of tea?'

He turned quickly. 'Sure.'

She was standing, hunched a little despite the warmth of the morning, the same shapeless grey cardigan pulled up about her throat, drawn down over her wrists. 'Come on then,' she said, and turned away.

He paused for a moment; he had expected that she would bring the tea out into the garden. There seemed to him a certain impropriety in social visits to the tenants' flats. But, all the same, he followed her into the dimness, along the corridor, and into the kitchen. The sudden cool-ness of the flat struck at the bare skin of his arms and shoulders, chilled the dampness of his sweaty singlet.

He sat at the tiny hinged table, fiddled with a cigarette,

while she lit the gas, filled the kettle, spooned tea into a cheap aluminium pot. He looked idly about the room. It seemed still anonymous, bare. There was little evidence of her occupancy; odd plastic canisters, a few cheap jars, a small transistor radio, a couple of threadbare tea-towels.

She poured the tea, fetched the milk from the tiny refrigerator, opened a screw-capped jar half filled with lumpy sugar.

He sipped, relaxing a little, aware of some impending break in the wall of her indifference. But he sensed, too, a struggle in her, a hint of that effort he had felt before, the effort she seemed to find necessary to admit outsiders to the private world behind her eyes.

Before he had half finished his tea, hot and weak, she spoke. She looked, not at him, but down at her own cup, chaliced in her thin hands. Carlo noticed, with a sudden stab of something like tenderness, that the two little fingers were slightly curved, bowed, a curious parenthesis.

'Listen,' she said, 'you told me if there was anything ...'

The pause lengthened.

'Yes?' he said, at last curious.

'Well,' she said, 'it's not a job or anything ...' She raised her eyes suddenly to his, and before she looked down again he caught the quick tremor of some desperate urgency. 'The thing is, I'm a bit light on for the rent. I wondered, could you lend me ten bucks? I'd pay you back next week for certain ...'

'Sure.' He was taken aback, embarrassed at her need, and somehow disappointed. He reached quickly into the hip pocket of his shorts, found nothing there. 'My wallet's in the ute ... I'll get it.' He stood up quickly, and walked out into the warmth and light of the morning. In the parking lot he reached through the window into his coat pocket, opened his wallet, pulled out a note. Turning, he was surprised to find her standing close behind him, and he almost bumped into her. He fumbled the money into her hand.

'Thanks,' she said. 'Next week … for sure.'

'No worries. On the dole?'

She nodded quickly and turned to go, hesitated. 'You want some more tea?'

He was sure she expected, hoped for, a refusal. And with some relief he shook his head. 'I better get on with it.'

Her sneakers made no sound as she drifted across the concrete and down the steps, out of sight.

It was three days to rent day, he knew. No mates, he thought, and she must be nervous.

A little later, burning rubbish in the far corner of the garden, he saw her hurry up the steps, climb into the VW; heard the engine grind reluctantly to life. The car reversed into the street, narrowly missing the gatepost, and disappeared. He listened as its uncertain cough slowly faded.

At lunch time he went to a pub half a mile away for a beer. When he returned he saw that the VW was back in its place. There was no sign of the girl. But towards evening, when the sun was striking deeply into the tiny box of her porch she came out and sat on the concrete floor, back against the wall, legs stretched straight in front of her. As he passed, going towards his utility, sweat cooling and drying, he saw that her eyes were closed. They opened slowly as he passed, and he saw that they were somehow different; less darkness in them, lighter, wider. She smiled at him, said nothing, just smiled, easily, gently. He noticed that, despite the late-afternoon warmth, the grey cardigan was still drawn tightly up to her throat, the ends of the ragged sleeves tucked into her loosely clenched fists. She closed her eyes again, her face open as a flower in the late sun.

Driving away, it occurred to him suddenly that the next Tuesday was a long way off.

The next week the door to number three was closed again, dark and blank as ever. Mrs Sykes, on her way to the supermarket, saw him looking at it.

'Won't see *her* yet a while,' she said, a thin scornful edge to her voice.

'Oh?'

'Resting up, I reckon. Doesn't look too strong, you know, I s'pose all the night work's taking it out of her ...'

'Got a job, then, has she?'

Mrs Sykes gave him a single pitying glance as she straightened a pink plastic curler and swung away up the steps. 'More like a profession, I'd say ...'

Carlo watched her go, frowning a little, then began unloading trays of petunias.

An hour later Mrs Sykes was back. 'Come and have a cuppa,' she called to him as she passed. 'No cooking today, that bastard Charlie's taking me out to eat tonight, even if he doesn't know it yet ...'

He sat on the steps that led to her chrome and laminex kitchen, a kitchen crammed with gadgetry indulgences. Eating sweet bought biscuits and drinking tea, he half-listened to her easy chatter. But all the time he was wondering about the closed door of number three. When he was released by Mrs Sykes he felt relieved, and went quickly back to work, finding a place from which he could observe the door. It's the ten dollars, he thought; I'm not getting done for a tenner just because she lays those big sad eyes on me. But he had a habit of honesty; and knew quite well that there was more to it than that.

He did not see her that day, nor the next week.

On the following Tuesday he considered knocking on her door. But if he did, and she hadn't the money, they would both be embarrassed. And even if she had it, he realized, they would still be embarrassed. So he waited, glancing almost furtively at the door from time to time, aware of growing tension and uneasiness inside himself. It wasn't the money at all; he accepted that now. He had faced the fact, had written it off, discounted it in his mind, weeks ago.

And had almost given up hope of seeing her again. Only the sight of the red VW in the car-park reassured him of her continuing presence in the closed flat.

So he was surprised when, early on a Tuesday morning a month later, she ran, a little breathless, from her door. It was summer, now, and in the full heat and glare she seemed frailer than ever, a wraith floating in her strange long dress and threadbare cardigan. Her paleness was startling beside his deepening tan.

Quickly she pushed a note into his hands.

'I'm sorry,' she said. 'Sorry I was so long about it.'

'That's all right.' He felt awkward, wanting suddenly to touch her, to run a single blunt finger over the fine skin of her cheek. But she had retreated, stood a safe three paces away, watching him with eyes brighter, bluer, livelier, than he remembered.

'Come and have some tea,' she said. 'Later, after I've been shopping.'

'OK.'

She backed away, smiling, then turned and ran lightly towards the dark tunnel of her doorway.

A little later he saw her again, moving quickly up the steps to the car-park. She waved at him, and he raised a hand.

He ate his lunch in the car-park, reluctant to leave in case he missed her return; then went back thirsty to work. The afternoon dragged on interminably as he went about the garden chores, waiting. Finally he took the shears and went to work on the west side of the building, out of sight of the car-park, a conscious rebellion against his new and disturbing dependence. But all the time his ears strained for the sound of the returning VW. It didn't come, and at last he gave up. At five o'clock he packed his tools and left, driving out of the car-park feeling hurt and let-down, and angry at himself because of it.

But he waited for several minutes at the corner in the vain hope of seeing her return.

The weeks passed, the solstice and its celebrations came and went, the heat grew, white dust drifted in from the road and settled on the parching leaves of the peach, the apple trees, the quince. Fruit ripened, the ground grew dry and powdery, and Carlo spent more time watering, weeding, mulching. Sometimes, on very hot days, he came in the evenings, to water the beds. The carnations were in full bloom now, filling the air with their cinnamon scent.

Carlo watched, but saw her only once. She came, late one evening, when the fading day was returning shadow and colour to the garden. He heard the old car lurch through the gate, and saw the familiar battered bonnet quiver to a stop. She was halfway down the steps before she saw him. For a brief moment she paused, then went on, hunching her shoulders a little, looking downward at the hot concrete where her sneakers scattered whispers of dust.

'Hi,' he said.

'Hi …' She raised one hand a little, a half-wave, and kept going. He watched the door close behind her, and turned away.

She seemed thinner, he thought, as if she were being somehow drained.

The summer crept slowly over the land like a slow bright cloud, leaching the colour from the trees, the sky. Only the fruit, the flowers, grew daily brighter. And as the season faded, so, thought Carlo, did the girl. He caught only brief glimpses of her, now; she seemed intent on avoiding him, and when she could not avoid his presence, avoided the open concern in his eyes. On the few occasions when they met she scurried like some frightened animal to the dark shelter of her flat.

At last, on a day of heat and lowering cloud, a day when sweat started as easily as weeds, he conquered his commonsense, his best judgement, and knocked on the glass panel of the door. She was there, he knew; the VW was in the car-park.

But the sound of his knocking echoed emptily, again and again, beyond the door.

He almost turned away, but at the last moment, in a panic of resolution, he twisted the knob ... and the door opened.

Inside, the passage was as dim as ever, as musty, an oppression of thick stale air.

He walked slowly past the kitchen, past the bedroom with its unmade bed and untidy scattering of clothes; found her in the living room at the end of the corridor. The blinds were drawn, and she lay on the shabby vinyl sofa by the left wall, facing him. He stopped in the doorway, motionless, looking at her.

'Go away,' she said, 'please.'

He walked to the sofa, stood looking down at her. She was shivering a little, her nostrils red and raw, her eyes swimming and dark in bruised valleys. He sat down beside her on the edge of the sofa, feeling the slight weight of her hips against him. Despite the heat she wore the old grey cardigan. Slowly he reached out and picked up her left hand, the one that lay nearest him. She tried to pull away, a movement so weak that it seemed a hardly discernible reflex. Only in her eyes was there a firm strength to her resistance.

'Please,' she said.

With his other hand he slipped the sleeve of her cardigan up her arm until it was above the elbow. For a long moment he looked at the dead-white skin, then gently drew down the sleeve again to cover the needle marks. When he looked back at her eyes again he could see nothing there but pain; and wasn't sure whose pain it was — hers, or his own, reflected in the dark hollows.

'What is it?' he said. 'Smack?'

She lay silent, her eyes fixed blankly beyond him.

'Word games,' he said. 'Funny, we talked about word games once. *El clavo*, remember? It means something else, too … a bummer, you know, a bad trip, something that gives you the shits …' Shit, he thought without humour, up to your eyeballs in it …

Still she said nothing. He watched the faint veins throbbing gently in her naked throat, starving in the heavy grey light.

'Go away,' she said at last, her voice small and very tired. 'Please.'

He stood up, went out into the bathroom. It wasn't there; nor in the bedroom. He found it, at last, in the kitchen; an old chocolate tin hidden clumsily in the cutlery drawer. Inside it lay the deadliness of the wasp-sharp hypodermic, the tie, the discoloured spoon. There was nothing else — no bag, not even an empty one. He put the tin back in its place, returned to the living room. She hadn't moved.

'Can't you score?' he asked.

She moved her head, a slow side-to-side motion of almost indifferent hopelessness.

He sat down again beside her, lifted her hand, held it clasped between his large calloused palms. She made no move to withdraw it, lay staring tiredly up at the cracked map of the ceiling.

'You haven't got a job,' he said. 'And you're not tough enough to be ripping stuff off. So you're hawking it, right?'

She said nothing, lifted her other hand to wipe her nose.

'Doesn't have to be like this, you know,' he said.

For a moment she dropped her eyes, looked at him, and he saw in them a curious emptiness that frightened him. But he ploughed on. 'You *can* get off it, you know...'

'How would you know?'

He was surprised at the coldness, the immense bitterness, in a voice so faint and distanced.

'Ever tried?' he asked. 'Cold turkey?'

After a long pause she shook her head, faintly, dismissively.

'I'll tell you something,' he said. 'It never killed anyone yet. It's bloody awful, I know... But it never killed anyone.'

She sighed then, deeply, tiredly. 'Please,' she said, 'just fuck off, will you? I know you're a nice bloke, but please fuck off ...'

For what seemed a long time he sat beside her, cupping the thin petal of her palm, gently stroking the soft skin of her wrist with his thumbs, as if trying to massage a little of his rude strength into the ruin of her flesh.

'If you want,' he said, 'we could try.' And realized in a sudden swooping that was close to nausea, the enormity of his commitment. 'I could come every day. In the mornings, at lunchtime, at night. At the weekend.' He paused. 'That's all it would take. A week. I'd bring you some flagons of wine ... it's a help ... you could make it ... I know.'

Slowly she closed her eyes. 'Go away now,' she said. 'Please, I really want you to go now...'

For a moment he thought that he felt a slight pressure, a warmth, in her fingers. He waited, but there was only the faint pulse of her blood.

'All right.' He stood up, releasing her fingers, letting them flow like water from his hands. 'But ... if you change your mind, just tell me. Any time.'

She nodded faintly.

For one more long and clumsy moment he stood there, his limbs seeming to grow strangely larger, more gross and useless. Then he wheeled quickly away and plunged out through the door, back down the narrow passage towards the heaviness of the hot grey day that lay waiting for him.

Mrs Sykes, pegging out her washing, gave him a thin glance as he clumped past her.

Wordlessly, he began grubbing out fading plants from the dry soil.

The weeks dragged slowly for him. In the evenings, on his way home from work, he often found himself going out of his way to drive past the flats. Sometimes the VW was in the car-park, sometimes not. He never stopped.

And, on Tuesdays, he never went near the closed door again. But it seemed to him that a kind of ache bled through the plain green panels of the door, the dark pebbled glass, stirring a dull answering pain inside him.

He never saw her, and there was no sign, no appeal.

But he waited.

In the coolness of a morning at the beginning of autumn he set out the trays of plants, dug and raked the bed, preparing. The sunlight, even at mid-morning, was cooler now on his naked back. Soon it would be time for a shirt again.

'Did you hear?' asked Mrs Sykes, leaning from her window, nibbling at a Chocolate Royal. 'About her?' She jerked the bright paisley of her rayon turban in the direction of number three.

Carlo stared blankly at her, shook his head.

'Found her on the weekend, they did.' She pursed her lips round crumbs of sticky chocolate; chewed, swallowed. 'On drugs, they said. You know, heroin or something ...'

'Where is she?'

'Gone,' said Mrs Sykes. 'Dead. You know, an overdose ...'

Carlo lowered himself slowly to his knees, rested his

knuckles gently on the gritty soil, looking downward at the sudden strangeness of his blunt hands so that she would not see his face.

'Why do they do it?' said Mrs Sykes, reaching behind her for another biscuit. 'They must know it'll kill them ...'

'I don't know,' said Carlo, watching his fingers crumble small clods of soil. A surge of grief and pity swept over him, an almost unbearable weight of darkness that seemed to suffocate him. Yet under the grief, the pity, he felt the beginning of a sickness start in his belly and rise towards his throat, a sickness at the unspeakable guilt of his own relief. For some charge had been taken from him. He felt suddenly light-headed and dizzy at the immensity of his betrayal.

He reached blindly into the tray beside him and dug out a cluster of plants.

'What are you planting?' asked Mrs Sykes.

'French marigolds,' said Carlo, staring down at the tiny plants.'For the winter.'

'That's nice,' said Mrs Sykes. 'A little bit of colour for the dull days.' She swallowed the last of her biscuit, withdrew her head and closed the window.

Carlo began to scoop small holes for the marigolds, spacing the plants neatly a hand's-breadth apart in the waiting earth.

A Diminishing Balance

The heat of February echoing like an iron bell; summer's coda bursting from the sky, pulsing from the edges of a naked sun. Inside the glasshouse the humidity broke in the air like sweat as the tepid hose-water trickled over the dry concrete paving, splashed the pots of yellowing orchids, the weedy baskets of wilting ferns and begonias. The cracked and scummed panes held back a little of the blaze, but trapped, amplified, a core of heat.

Dead, he wished them dead, the plants. Dead, finally done with, gone, gone.

Yet they clung, tenuously, tenaciously, to life: and he was chained to their needs. Every few days — often enough, just often enough — he managed the walk to the bottom of the garden; leaned on the dirty fibro bench; hosed briefly against the intensity of the heat; kept a minimal kind of life struggling in the fading and bedraggled clumps. But, always, in the hot dampness his dizziness grew worse, his breathing clogged, and with each visit his stay grew briefer.

He dropped the hose, turned the tap, staggered a little on the cinder path, braced himself for the burning air that waited for him outside.

Conscience? No, some duty perhaps. Well, whatever, he felt it, a deep thing, too deep for understanding. But she had cared for the plants, and so now must he.

He moved slowly towards the back steps, the house.

White paint peeling and blistered, weatherboards show-
ing the bare grey grain of their old timber. Weeds, dry and
stubborn, bursting in the concrete cracks. He no longer
noticed.

Inside the house, a relative coolness. He passed through
the bare bright kitchen in which, now, he never cooked.
Only old stains marred the smeared walnut laminex, the
bloomed chromium.

Behind the kitchen door unremembered foodstains on
the wall. Old ones, later he would ...

Through the arch to the living room, green carpet studded with black cigarette burns like the husks of dead
insects. He lay down, easing himself onto the grubby white
vinyl of the sofa, lit a cigarette.

Forbidden, against orders. More tests next month. It
didn't seem to matter. Until some final knowledge.

In the silence a familiar uneasiness moved in him, stirring like slow fronds at the dark edge of a clear sea-pool.
But, avoiding examination, recognition, he slept, the half-
smoked cigarette dropping gently to smoulder slowly into
a new crater in the charred carpet.

He woke just before midday, grudgingly, to a deeper heat,
his mind hazed and thick with a confusion of images.

Figures, papers, lists. The plants. Lisa. He glanced at her
photograph on the small table. No children, no grand-
children, of his own. But a step-granddaughter at least.
Like the plants, to be preserved. But the names, the list.
A slow clearing of his mind, an emptiness in his belly at
the prospect of impossible urgencies.

He lay very still, listening to the roughness of his own
breathing in the silent shell of the house.

Already, already in his seventieth year. So quickly, it had
all gone so quickly. Dances, parties, all their friends.

Her father would get the house. Of course.

He reached for the packet, lit another cigarette, began

to recruit his distant energies. Lunch, food, habit. Soon, soon. But not yet.

As he gathered himself laboriously under the weight of burdens and the heat, thoughts of the papers returned, lodged themselves like some recurrent ache behind his eyes.

The list in the living room behind the record player. His bank book in the kitchen drawer. Lisa's in the bedroom, in the dressing table. In separate rooms, kept apart, always apart. To bring them together would be, somehow, a kind of admission that he refused to make.

Half an hour later he left the house; shaved, heavy-bellied in new drip-dry shirt, fresh slacks, second-best panama. With a bottle of beer sweating coldly in one hand he walked to the carport, treading carefully from shadow to narrow shadow, avoiding the hammering of the sun.

He rested in the car for a moment, eyes closed, head back.

Thinking: in good shape, she's in good shape, only 26,000 on the clock. A few burns here and there, but in good shape. *Hers*, it had been hers, his old Austin long gone; the old car, the rented flat, the storeman's wage.

Thinking: company, though, I gave her company, friends, parties, good fun, the things she needed.

A stabbing recollection of the figures, a sudden dryness in his mouth: he hurried to turn the key.

He drove two blocks, past raffia-dry nature strips, past the knotted fists of hard-cropped elms, past old houses racked with renovations and artificial brick, his progress in the car as hesitant and uncertain as it had been on foot. He hardly heard the mutter of the main street's traffic, even with his hearing aid on full gain.

Lunch, lunch was one of the pegs on which he hung his days.

Old friends, Arthur and Mary. At all their parties in those days.

No more. Everything running down now. No more parties, no more dancing.

Salad, Mary would have salad, he knew.

Parking in their driveway, carefully. Thinking, three years and no dents in the car, none at all.

Eating his salad slowly, crisp fragments edging under his plate, he drank his beer and talked a little with Arthur. Of the heat, of bowls, of old friends. But the talk was fragmented, half Arthur's words lost; and it was not only his atrophied hearing that separated them, but his fractured thoughts.

Remembering, through the flavour of smooth mayonnaise and sharp sour beer, bowls. Three years, three summers since he had played. Still, they all knew him, remembered. Skip five years in a row. Gave his bowls away. To someone. Who? The young postman, perhaps. He couldn't remember. One day he would go and watch. Have a drink. But when it was cooler. Autumn, then.

With half his beer undrunk, halfway through an unheard sentence, he left.

Back in the house he lay again on the white sofa. Under the weight of the afternoon he slipped almost imperceptibly in and out of sleep, waking at intervals to the prickings of the same stale and familiar dilemma. Once he rose painfully and made his way to the record player, brought out the list — a list scrawled haphazardly in mismatched inks on an old piece of cardboard. And as he held it in his stubby mottled fingers, looked from name to name, from address to address, he felt a rising desperation, almost a physical nausea.

Thinking: too late, it's too late.

Putting back the list, thinking, there's always the house ...

But that must be preserved. Money was one thing, but

the house, no, it was bound somehow, must go intact to Terry. Like the plants, to be preserved. Terry didn't like him. But he had promised. The car, then. But he needed the car. In the autumn, the trips, the necessary trips. The pension? Its paucity frightened him.

Lying on the sofa again the still quiet afternoon closed over him. Dim, almost cool. He would not move, he decided, until evening came.

In the late afternoon he woke again. And for a moment felt almost hopeful. Rose and took out the list again.

Perhaps a short trip. A phone call, even. Then to follow it up …

He looked at the list.

Northcote, Victoria.

Impossible.

Stafford, Queensland.

Worse.

He checked off the closer names. The nearest was a hundred miles away. His brief hope fell away, leaving the faint familiar tremors. The injustice of it seemed suddenly to choke him. Any of them, any one of them, he could make any one of them happy. Company, parties, dancing, the things they needed. Well, when he felt a little better. Next month. The doctor, after the doctor, after that.

He put away the list once more, walked a little unsteadily to the kitchen drawer, the one crammed with papers: bills, receipts, old letters. In sudden bravado he took out his bank book. Three years ago, a balance of sixteen thousand. Now only $134 left. He dropped the book back in the drawer, closed it quickly, feeling the bitterness inside him almost like a reassurance.

Without knowing quite how he came to be there, he found himself in the front room, facing the cocktail cabinet. On the mirrored top a gallon flagon of scotch stood pot-bellied in a cluster of gold-rimmed glasses. He poured, drank quickly. But the liquor rose implacably in his throat on a tide of bile. He ran, stumbling, and halfway to the bathroom vomited on the oyster-grey carpet in the hall.

No use, only beer, now he could drink only a little beer. Nothing was left, nothing.

He lay down again, the taste of whiskied vomit a new accusation on his tongue.

In the evening he showered slowly, carefully, no longer daring to sit in the tub. Chose another new shirt, put on his green bowling-club blazer and best panama. Drove six blocks in third gear to the Gentlemen's Club. There were no doctors among the members now, no dentists, no solicitors. But all the better for that. Friendlier. People knew him, spoke to him. Joe, good old Joe, skip for five years in a row, always good for a laugh, always a story on tap. He settled in his seat by the window, ordered chops, a bottle of beer.

But with the meal half-eaten, the beer half-drunk, three cigarettes stubbed out half-smoked, he found that a great tiredness had crept over him. And his breath seemed shorter. Almost painful.

And the club was quiet. No friends tonight.

He called to the waiter, signed the chit. As he did so the nightmare of the diminishing balance in his bank book flashed at him with the vivid shock of an unexpected dirty postcard. He swallowed quickly, fearing nausea, and edged slowly out of the dining room into the car-park.

A quiet evening at home.

But they were all quiet evenings at home now.

And in the dusk, brightly polished shoes crunching on crisp gravel, a little truth overtook him gently, a half-expected guest arrived at last.

Truth. He had never looked ahead, not really. Had avoided it, evaded it. Life had always worked out. And never wondering about it at all, really. Jessie's death, the sorrow, he still felt it, after thirty years. But life went on when you were left behind. The money had lasted almost until he had met Alice.

And they had had a good sharing, too, he knew.

But three years now, looking after things. The plants, the house.

Well, a bit of paint, some cleaning, nothing much needed. Soon, soon he would do it.

Never a bludger, he'd never been that. Thinking: I always paid my way, one way or another. But it had all gone so fast. Everything went so fast.

A little time, that was all.

In the silent house he switched on all the lights. Their brightness seemed to hold back a creeping emptiness that came with the night. He walked slowly from room to room, uneasy. Over the last years the small night sounds — the distant drone of traffic, the hum of the refrigerator, the rustle of leaves — had grown progressively so attenuated to his ears that their final extinction had passed without notice. But tonight a different kind of silence seemed locked in the core of the house, a silence quite independent of his deafness.

He peered out through the screen door. Clouds were gathering over the familiar serrations of the western hills, and he could see the harsh blades of the cabbage palm rattling soundlessly in the wind. Perhaps rain, he thought. But more likely not.

He turned away, walked back into the living room.

The books, all the books.

He had been tempted, often, to get rid of them; to send them to Terry, to give them to him on one of the rare occasions when he brought Lisa on a visit. After all, they had belonged to Terry's father. But always something had stopped him. Terry, he knew, had never liked him. Had been unhappy when Alice had left him the house, the money. Not that Terry needed them. He never understood Terry, thought him perhaps the same kind of man his father had been.

His father, the man of the books. Books that carried names he had never heard of. Sholokov. Pap. Russell. Saroyan. Hemingway. Lin Yutang. And other ones, strange ones, with titles he could not even understand.

He had never opened them. Even had they interested him, it would have seemed somehow improper.

And Alice had never read. How had she put up with it for thirty years?

And the music, classical music, he never even looked at the old records in the back of the racks, couldn't remember the names. How had she? So fond of jazz and dancing. A kind of joyful warmth ...

And the pictures were gone, the pictures of the man of the books and the music. It had been some kind of unspoken agreement.

But the books remained, a puzzle, dumb and constant.

Tonight, though, the strange man, fifteen years dead, seemed suddenly closer. He felt almost a kind of understanding. A quietness — controlled, taut, unyielding. Like the night.

But no parties, no dancing. How *had* she?

He turned on the colour TV.

And remembered that the rental was due at the end of the month.

Well, he would manage. Somehow. It was all, now, that filled his nights.

But on this night the colours jarred, and he could see strange flat patches of make-up on the mouthing faces of the strangers. He turned up the volume until the sound boomed and rattled tinnily through the house. Yet he could barely hear the dialogue.

No contact, no meaning. He had forgotten even the

name of the programme. He laboured to his feet again, switched off the set.

Something familiar. Something of old times, old friends.

On his way to the record rack he was taken with a sudden shortness of breath, clutched a chairback, held there grimly for a minute, for two or three, as he struggled with the bilges of his lungs.

No pain, though. A good sign.

At the record rack, one hand grasping the flaked gilding, he riffled through the bright covers.

Winifred Atwell. Gordon MacRae. She had liked Gordon MacRae.

Nelson Eddy and Jeannette MacDonald, favourites, and they had sung late-night duets. His own voice good and true, hers flat. He had never told her.

His fingers stopped at the familiar orange cover. *The 'R' Certificate Songbook.* ADULTS ONLY. They had played it at all the parties. This same room, crowded, Arthur and Mary, Enid and George, Jean and Harry, all of them. She had laughed high and loud, drunk too much cherry brandy and lemonade, sung flat with the rude songs. They had all sung them, all good sports, late at night, a little drunk, no longer young. But happy enough, a kind of family feeling, a closeness, a sharing ...

He slid the record from its sleeve, put it on the turntable, stepped back carefully to the deep padded chair, sank into the cracking vinyl, listening. Volume turned up, but not too far. It was too early, and the neighbours.

Anyway, he remembered them all so well, a phrase, a word now and then was all he needed, he knew them by heart ...

'The Woodpecker's Hole'. Arthur knew more verses than the record, could sing them all night.

'The Bastard King of England'. That odd slow melody at the beginning. Something he knew, but couldn't quite remember. Nothing to do with the song. But he knew it, from somewhere ...

But *her* favourite, this one.

His foot tapped soundlessly in the loose pile of the charred carpet as the raucor of the repetitive obscenities echoed through the empty rooms.

... he was lousy and dirty and covered in fleas and the hair on his balls hung down to his knees. God bless the Bastard King of England ...

... Rule Britannia, marmalade and jam, five *Chinese* crackers upyourarsehole bang-bang bang-bang *bang* ...

His fingers tapping happily, hopelessly unsynchronized, on the chair-arm. Eyes closed, he forgot, almost, the labouring of tired and flooding lungs, the urgencies held at bay by the barrier of the nostalgic ribaldries. He no longer heard, even in his mind, the record; only the voices of those nights when they had all sung together, all been a little drunk, all been close and secure and — for a time — unafraid.

He listened past the end of the record, no longer conscious of anything except that world that lay beyond the limits of atrophied eardrums and run-down hearing-aid batteries.

Fingers tapping, toe beating the air.

Some of the songs he skipped, shutting them off without effort. Some forgotten, some never liked, or never fully understood.

But hearing, again and again, all the voices ...

But 'The Bastard King of England', her favourite.

Eyes closed, the record long run out, the faint hiss of the speakers inaudible to his frozen eardrums, he sat; rapping, toe-tapping, singing it all over in his head, the indelible verses, the talismans, the charms, that had held them safe. For that time.

... lousy and dirty and covered in fleas and the hair on his balls hung down to his knees ...

... Rule Britannia, marmalade and jam, five *Chinese* crackers upyourarsehole, bang-bang, bang-bang, *bang* ...

He slept at last, uneasily, in the hard bright light of his private silence.

Woke much later from a strange dream of childhood, of the smell of plums, of the opening bars of the song, the part he could never identify.

Tiredly, he gathered himself, followed the pressure of his bladder to the bathroom; saw as he passed the mirror in the hall that he was still wearing his panama hat, his best one, the brim creased where it had rested, crushed, against the chairback. He removed it, tried to straighten it, smoothing ineffectually at the irreparable cracks in the delicate weave. Sighed, dropped it on top of the dirty-linen basket.

In bed, he lay with the lamp lit, letting his breathing quieten slowly. Flicked at his stainless-steel lighter, tried a final cigarette, but stubbed it out as the coughing began and he felt the rattle of the fluids in his chest, a tired wheezing gurgle.

Tomorrow.

But first a good night's sleep.

Tomorrow he would get up early, water the plants. Perhaps make a phone call. Then, in a week or so, when he was better ...

He coughed a little, carefully, then switched off the light.

Sleep came, as it came always now, slowly; he drifted for a time on a wave that dipped him at last into a doze filled with old songs and bank books and the remembered taste of clean black rum ...

Waking, sweating in the darkness, at 3 a.m. To breathe was

like the beginnings of drowning: first, the effort not to inhale, to hold off the enemy air as long as possible; then finally, surrender, and the struggle against his lungs, lungs locked solid in a pulpy bubbling. He lay in the wide warm bed, racked and hawking, craving sleep, wanting only to avoid the slow terrors of conscious breathing. But unable yet to bring himself to wish not to wake next morning. There were duties still, promises to keep.

But nothing had prepared him, no one had told him. Not about this.

Streetlights flushed at the edges of the drawn venetians. He lay for a long time staring at the faint shadows on the ceiling. The nervous burden of wakefulness ran in small tremors through his limbs, and he fumbled a cigarette from the packet on the night table. Lit it, seeing the room flare suddenly at him in the orange glow; seeing it as if for the first time, framed by the crags and bony caverns of his eyes, the promontory of his nose.

A glass of rum, dark and heavy, to bring sleep. But his gorge rose even as the wish came. Thinking of the great flagon of whisky, almost untouched, in the front room. Terry would get it, or Arthur.

What? No, *he* would drink it. After the doctors. Next month.

He coughed again, slowly, heavily, in hawking half-retches, and stubbed out the cigarette, lay still after the final spasm, in lone and ultimate abandonment, the last pleasure gone. And condemned to the long dark hours till morning.

He could feel it edging at him, the need to see, to confirm it once more. To feel, to weigh the tangible guilt of the heavy blue pages in his fingers. Somehow it always seemed to ease him.

He switched on the light.

On the way to the dressing table he stumbled once, then stood there, leaning, stocky and thick-bellied in his flannel pyjamas. Sucked in his breath slowly, as if lifting a great weight.

The drawer jammed once, and he shook it free impatiently. From beneath the leather box of cuff-links, the pile of neatly laundered handkerchiefs, he drew out the blue bank book. Turned it in his hands, opened it.

In Trust for Lisa Slocombe.

In trust.

The note slipped between the pages. *Her* writing, the familiar scrawl; always practical, presuming accurately her own disaster.

Joe, I have lent Molly $2,000 from Lisa's account. She will pay it back over the next year or so.

Molly, her sister. And she *had* paid it back. In money orders to him. Cashed. Spent. The last entry in the book was the withdrawal, four years old. The balance stood, as it had then, at $500.

Later, he had thought, each time the money orders came. Later.

There had always been something, some unexpected expense. But he *would* put it back. When he was better, when he could get about, see people. One of them, it would be all right ...

Time, only time.

But his own account — $134.

The car, he could sell the car. But then he couldn't travel, see them ...

Mortgage the house.

Impossible. The house must be kept, free, intact. To be preserved, passed on.

Money. Time. Money.

Standing barefooted in the thick carpet, cold now in the warm night, he thought again about his own death; found, strangely, that he had no fear of it now, not of the physical cessation, of the dissolution of his body. But the vision of the final stripping terrified him: he would be left bared, exposed to the world, to Terry, to Lisa. Naked, guilty, his remembrance a scornful thing. In his mouth, lying at the root of his tongue like some unhatched serpent, he felt the shape of the word.

Thief.

But not if he could …

A remaking. He would remake things, replace the money, everything would be as it was. Time, and somehow the money would come. Someone quieter this time, perhaps, less interested in parties, dancing. He would do his part, he knew his value, his use and purpose.

Strangely, the blue pages, the evidence of his most scarifying transgression, soothed and calmed him. After this there was nothing worse to be faced. And confronted by the last inescapable necessity he felt almost at peace, in control, resolved.

He put the book away, padded back to bed, switched out the light, and lay quietly. They would come back, the old faces, the good times. The book would be replenished, the account balanced. It would all come back. Loud music late at night. The old kindnesses, the laughter. She always tried to sing, always flat, but he had never told her. 'The Bastard King of England', and she always hummed the strange melody at the beginning, thinking it was part of the song. It wasn't really, he knew that. Could almost remember its name. Almost …

In the morning he would get up while it was still early, easy breathing in the coolness, water the plants properly. Out of place, it was out of place, the piece at the beginning. He knew it, his sister had sung it under the greengage tree sixty years ago.

Sunwarm plums long dry grass the tall rusty docks the smell of crushed fruit heady as liquor   and who   and who   and who but my Lady Greensleeves …

Smiling a little, breath rattling less urgently, he drifted

into a kind of sleep; a sleep where desperations were no longer focused on his failing body, where purposes were clear and unclouded, where he could still think kindly of the world he would remake, of the man he would become again ...

But his intentions were subverted, once more, by his failing body. He overslept, waking only when the day was already drowning in heat, the empty air ringing like some warning in his deaf ears.

Sweating, empty-bellied, his head light and unballasted, he made his erratic way to the glasshouse. It seemed suddenly important now that the plants survive in some greater measure of security. But his resolution carried him only a few paces past the door; there, the familiar weariness caught him and he leaned against his usual bench. A mistiness, as of light steam after summer rain, seemed to rise from the floor, wisping across his vision. He blinked his eyes. Directly confronting him, no more than a pace away, a shrivelled and straggling orchid, suspended from the roof truss, clung by a mass of pale thin roots to a slab of dry tree-fern. From the centre of the tangle a thin spike of green drove towards the sun, a dozen tiny spotted yellow buds swaying slightly in the slow drift of air from the doorway.

A big spike, he thought, with vague memories of the plant's flowering in earlier, better, years. Bigger than last year.

And he remembered what she had once told him — that dying orchids threw all their energies into a final prodigal burst of flowering, a frantic effort to seed the world with the beginnings of a new generation.

And then died.

One final burst, he thought. Give me one final burst. And don't let me be alone ...

Soon, soon, he thought. Soon I'll go, when the weather is cooler ... I'll find her, whoever she is, and it can all be put right, it can all begin again, everything as it was ...

But he sensed suddenly, with a great emptiness clutching at his bowels, that already the threads had been drawn too tight; that he had arrived at some point where there remained no longer any possibility of reversal, of delay, of postponement; that in the span of a single day his grip on life had grown as tenuous as that of the dying orchid. Fear closed over him, a sudden darkness under the sunlight, and he found that he could hardly bear the knowledge that burst so suddenly on him. Saw with quick terror, just as he saw the diminishing balance in the bank books and the encroaching weakness of his body, the final truth, the last and long-evaded truth. That at the core of him, in the depths where he had always counted on a certain quality, he was eroded totally; that inside the shell of flesh that he had carried so laboriously through the days and nights there remained now no last trace of substance; that the balance of his life had been wasted as remorselessly as had that of the bank books; that it no longer mattered even about the books, about tomorrow. Because now there was nothing of him remaining; his life was, finally, a nullity, a void.

The terror of his own emptiness took him, seized him, shook him as the wind might shake the last empty pod on a barren tree.

And recognizing, accepting, the immanent extinction of his own foundering body — an extinction as meaningless as the collapse of the struggling orchid — he felt a new horror, beyond even the foreknowledge of his posthumous shame, begin to gnaw at the new rawness of his mind. For he saw clearly now that when the end came he must face oblivion with no companion but his own self-revulsion; that in the last moments of breath he would be twinned indivisibly with a stranger whom he knew suddenly too well.

And so stood, motionless, at the end of more than summer, biting on his new and bitter knowledge as if on some dark bullet that might blunt the edge of his ultimate pain.

A Pale Wolf in Winter

Sweating gently under our oilskins, the rhythm easy by the third day. Snow hard-crusted underfoot, packs setting easily. Making better time than in summer, the rocks and tussocks three feet below our boots.

But not many make the trip in winter. Two weeks in a world of white, and no rescue choppers if you break a leg.

— Ainsworth, said Jess, and I looked up to see the ragged cup of the peak through a gap in the mist.

I looked at my watch. Three o'clock, and dark in an hour.

— What do you think? I said. Camp at Webster's Kingdom?

He nodded and turned a shade eastward, heading for the valley hidden beyond the next height of land. An early night, an early start in the morning. Ten miles down to the cairn, leave a note in the vegemite jar. A good trip, a clear trip. If the weather held. If it didn't storm, didn't thaw. Either way we'd hole up and wait. In summer they graze stock on the high plains, and there are shelters if you know where to find them.

— Bad weather coming, said Jess, jerking his head at the western horizon.

The sun behind a thin overcast, off-white and hazy. But at the horizon a band of livid yellow, rimming the edge of the plateau. Well, the Kingdom was as good a place as any to wait it out.

— When do you think? asked Jess.

— Before morning. Maybe midnight.

Sloping on down the incline, lengthening our stride a little.

In the lee of the mountain, a long cirque valley, flat and dead white. The burnt bones of trees thrusting up through the snow on the narrow valley sides, the tops of a few snow gums the only softness in a cold bare land. Beyond the end of the valley a glimpse of Wild Dog Mountain before a snow-squall swept down and we bowed our heads under the weight of the wind, pulling balaclava peaks down against the sudden drive of flakes that bit like hard-whipped sand.

Coming down to Webster's Kingdom in a flurry, low cloud sweeping in with the snow, the light fading in a hazed grey monochrome.

Tucked hard in against a spur, backed into a stand of pencil pine, stood the old hut; low, ramshackle, propped against the wind by a row of sagging spars, and banked already almost to the roof. But dry and almost snowtight. And the door, facing east, a good place for a fire.

We shed our packs, raked away the drift, and before first full dark had a fire, a billy boiling, hot food.

— How long will it last? said Jess, tapping the billy.

It was getting colder. Maybe fifteen, twenty below. And the wind backing sou'west.

— Two or three days, I said.

Sitting in a comfortable silence, not unpleased at the prospect of the time to be spent bound to the old hut. And thankful to old Webster, who had run cattle, scratched for osmiridium, built the shelter half a century ago, and whose bones lay on the western slope beyond the pines.

Night slipping over us like a dark blanket.

Thinking, nearly time to unroll the bags, crawl into the familiar warmth. Savouring the last of the fire, the dregs of hot bitter tea.

— Better hang the packs up, said Jess, the possums will be …

His strong voice fading abruptly, tailing off, and I looked up to see the black gap of his mouth in his fire-flickered face. Saw him staring past me into the darkness; followed his gaze, saw what he saw.

Standing there at the edge of the circle of firelight he looked so pale, insubstantial, that he might almost have been part of the snow, the shadows. A tall shambling figure that, as we watched, began to edge slowly towards us. We were on our feet by the time he reached the fire, and we could see that he was really tall. And so fair that he might have been an albino. Except for the pale-blue eyes. Curls of windburnt skin clung like hickory shavings to the patches of frostbite on his cheeks. A jut of narrow jaw, a long canine nose, thin fair hair matted with snow.

No cap. A kind of nylon yachting parka, serge ski trousers. Thin desert boots, no gaiters. A cheap, badly stowed pack hanging too low on his back. His legs dark, shining from the knees down.

Jess and I saw them at the same time.

— Jesus!

We hustled him to the fire, pulled at his boots and trousers. They crackled. We knew without asking what had happened. He'd gone too close to one of the frozen tarns, broken through the ice. His legs and feet were blue and mottled. We sat him down, started rubbing.

— Give him some tea, I said.

Neither of us had paid much attention to his face, but as Jess held the mug to his mouth we saw his eyes clearly for the first time. Pale, empty, distant.

I wondered how far gone he was. He looked almost happy, the long prow of his face pointing blindly into the sea of the night.

— In the pack, he said calmly. Bottle of rum.

Jess looked at me.

— Hell, I said, it can't make him any worse.

— I'm an auditor, said the stranger, his voice oddly low and thick for such a stringy frame. And he laughed, a sudden barking chuckle, deep and heavy. If that means anything, he said.

Jess found the bottle, poured rum into the tea.

— What the hell are you doing up there? I said. This is no country for a bloody winter bushwalk.

— I get to know things, he said. All kinds of things. But you can't do anything.

— What's your name? said Jess. Where do you come from?

— I come from the brothels, he said. Collins Street and Circular Quay …

Jess shook his head.

I rummaged in his pack. Nothing but a cheap sleeping bag and some canned food. No map, no matches, no clothing, nothing. I wrapped the bag around his shoulders and we wedged him between us in front of the fire.

— What'll we do with him? asked Jess.

— Keep him with us, I said. When the weather lets up we'll take him back in easy stages.

— Look at his feet, said Jess.

They were badly blistered. Blood seeped pink and watery onto the snow.

The stranger was silent then, for a long time, didn't seem to hear our questions. Just sat staring out into the darkness. The wind was a high wailing now in the pines. Out in the open it would be gusting to sixty or seventy knots.

We kept rubbing his legs until they lost most of their blueness. His toes looked bad, but there wasn't much we could do.

Suddenly he gave his strange doglike bark of laughter.

— Have you ever thought, he said, that we're choking on our own lives?

— What? said Jess.

— Choking, choking … every day a bit more, all that poison building up. You can't go on with it, you know …

And he swung the pale empty eyes from one of us to the other, his head swivelling slowly on the thin neck.

— There's a core, you know, he said. Nothing reaches it, nothing means anything deep down. Everything's outside. But all the outside things mount up, they bury you, choke you, the core gets smothered, and then it's no use anymore …

— Don't talk, said Jess. You're in shock.

He didn't seem to notice that Jess had spoken.

— You have to go back to the beginning, start thinking again in simple terms. Otherwise it's too confusing, too confusing. Got to be simple. Then you understand … clean and simple …

He lapsed into a long silence then. In profile the face seemed hatchet-narrow, beaked, aimed, trained on an infinity we couldn't see, nothingness beyond the raging of the storm.

Then the coughing laugh broke from his frame again, jerking out with a strength and vitality that mocked his frailness.

— I know what they do with their partly-owned subsidiaries, he said. I know how they siphon off the shareholders' funds before they show up in the profit and loss account …

And he peered at each of us in turn again, as if seeing us for the first time, trying to focus the pale eyes on us.

— You look like decent men, he said. Who are you?

— We're just farmers, said Jess.

— Ah, said the stranger, and hawked his heavy laughter into the night again. That explains it …

Later, as we wrapped him in an extra coat, zipped him into his sleeping bag, he spoke again.

— What's further on, to the south?

— Nothing said Jess. Fifty miles of nothing.

— Ah, said the stranger. He seemed almost lucid, then.

I lay for a long time in my sleeping bag, clutching my boots to my ribs to keep them from freezing, watching him in the last dying light from the fire. He lay motionless, eyes open, and seemed to be watching the snow drifting across the open door frame. That was the last I remember of him before I fell asleep.

I woke, thick with odd dreams, to bitter cold, Jess's hand shaking me.

— He's gone!

— What!

Jess played the dim beam of the torch, batteries frozen, on the empty sleeping bag. The pack, the extra coat, still lay there. But the thin boots and sodden trousers were gone, and the rum bottle.

I looked at my watch. Eleven o'clock. I'd slept three hours.

— How long? I said, fumbling into stiff boots.

— Not long, I heard him stumbling round outside …

We picked up his uncertain tracks in the lee of the hut. Heading round the spur, southward. At the edge of the pines the wind hit us, a numbing blast from the south-west. The snow stung like shot. And the footprints were already drifting over.

— Run, I said, and we broke into a clumsy canter through the powdery snow, up the slope towards the ridge. But halfway there we lost the tracks; they were already covered, buried, lost.

In the darkness and the aching cold we scrambled up the slope, buffeted and voiceless in the wind. All I could see was the loom of the ridge, Jess's bulk a dozen feet away.

At the top of the ridge the storm hit us with full force, and I stumbled, almost fell. Then Jess was beside me, mouth to my ear.

— What'll we do?

It was no good. From here on the wind curled and eddied off the face of the mountain, and within minutes we'd be lost.

— Nothing, I said dully. We'll look for him in the morning.

— Be dead in an hour, said Jess. Out in this …

— I know.

Then, suddenly, riding the wind the way a gull rides the waves, a neck-prickling sound swelled briefly through the night, somewhere to the south, distant, damped by the blanket of snow. It was — surely? — the sound of distant laughter; a short sharp bark that seemed to lift in pitch, echoing a loneliness as sharp and final as the howl of a dog-wolf heard across a dark lake.

And then it was gone, lost in the rush of snow flurries, the brutal force of the gale.

We waited on the ridge for longer than we should have, in case the sound should come again. But it didn't, and finally we retreated to the trees, the cold shelter of the hut, both our faces frost bitten.

Perhaps, after all, it wasn't him. Perhaps only a trick of the wind.

But there was that loneliness to the sound of it, and a strange accent of final triumph, that seemed somehow to echo the look I had seen in his eyes when he had asked, What's further on, to the south?

Nothing. Fifty miles of nothing.

I lay awake a long time, shivering in my bag, thinking about it, what it would be like out there. And wondering, the last thing before I slipped finally into sleep, if I would bring him back if I could …

The Last Sandwichman

He is the last one, the lone and final survivor of his tribe. Each day he walks through the crowded city streets, clamped between garish boards on breast and back; boards proclaiming electric organ demonstrations, cheap television rentals, stage shows, disposal sales, Christadelphian revivals, supermarket openings, sewing lessons.

In his face there is no acknowledgement of his solitary challenge to extinction; awareness, as in all extinctions, is sharpest in the eyes of the spectators.

He is tall, very thin, and his sparse grey hair is always combed neatly back from his pale face. He wears — you must think hard to remember — a blue serge coat, shiny grey trousers, narrow tie, worn black shoes. How old is he? Fifty-five? Sixty? He himself has difficulty remembering.

Have you ever wondered where he goes when, in the late afternoon, he sheds his boards for the day? No one seems to notice.

Not that there is any secret here. When he bends his knees, ducks his head beneath the shoulder straps, and emerges from his cardboard carapace he stacks the boards neatly in the corner of a small cleaners' room behind the town hall, smooths down his shiny serge, and steps out again into the city streets. For three blocks he walks south, his face as grey and empty as ever; he crosses the park, emerges into Charles Street, continues southward for two more blocks. At a huddle of crumbling terrace houses he turns aside, enters a narrow gate in a rotting picket fence. He takes out a key, opens a paint-blistered front door, crosses a dark hallway, climbs a steep smelly staircase, opens another door with another key ... and is home.

There are two rooms.

One is for eating, one for sleeping.

In the room for eating a sixty-watt globe has been burning continuously (except for power failures and interruptions for bulb replacements) for eleven years, five months, and nine days. That is how long he has lived here.

In the room there is a table, a kitchen chair, a cupboard, a sink, a small hotplate, an electric radiator, a transistor radio. And 6,241 gramophone records.

The records are all old 78s, bought in secondhand shops: Dame Clara Butt, Bing Crosby, Caruso, Jelly Roll Morton, Guy Lombardo, Kennerly Rumford, Fats Waller, Joe Loss, Fritz Kreisler, the Inkspots ...

In a corner there is an old-fashioned wind-up gramophone, but it no longer works. The spring broke shortly after he moved in. He has never bothered to have it repaired, finding in the end that he prefers silence.

There is a door at the far end of the room, next to the window, and through it lies the room for sleeping. In the sleeping room there is a bed, a wardrobe with a door that will not close properly, a chest of drawers with a wavy mirror the colour of dirty topaz, and 5,187 newspapers. On several occasions he has missed the daily paper owing to illness; but he has more than made up for the omissions by buying several papers each Sunday.

When he moved here — eleven years, five months, and nine days ago — he brought with him all his records. At that time there were 2,401 of them. He left behind 3,609 newspapers.

His housekeeping is simple. Once a week he makes his bed (he is a quiet sleeper), washes his clothes at the laundromat, sweeps his floor. He washes up when it is necessary, which is not often.

For breakfast each morning he eats two rounds of toast spread with margarine and jam, drinks two cups of weak tea.

He eats no lunch, but through the day sucks occasional peppermints.

On three evenings a week — Monday, Wednesday, and Friday — he buys fish and chips. On Tuesday evenings he buys a hamburger, on Thursday evenings a pizza. On Saturdays he buys dim sims or sweet and sour pork from the Chinese take-away. On Sundays he makes sandwiches with sliced meat and pickles.

When he comes home each evening he showers in the small bathroom across the corridor, eats, listens to the radio for a little while. Years ago the radio sometimes played records which he himself owned; but it seems no longer to happen. Later he reads the day's paper carefully, perhaps sorts through a pile or two of dusty records, goes to bed.

He never looks through the window. The blind was drawn when he moved in, and it is still drawn. He has no idea what lies outside the window, and does not care.

At weekends he sleeps a great deal. He goes out only to buy food and newspapers and, on Saturday mornings, to look for records in the secondhand shops.

He continues to acquire the records, the newspapers, only because — like listening to the radio — it is easier to go on than it is to stop. The fact of ownership no longer holds any meaning for him; possessions are phantoms, no more than ephemeral boundaries to a space already vacated.

He has no visitors.

He has no friends.

He has no name.

Oh, there are certain codes, certain labels, used by others. But for him his name is only a series of oddly arranged letters on an electoral roll, a taxation file, a census form. He has no use for it any more. Because a name is a tool with a function, a purpose; you use it, as you might dig the flukes of an anchor into sand, to check your drift. And he has no need to fix himself in a world that no longer exists.

You see him in the streets, you are aware of his presence; but always he seems to remain somehow faceless, featureless. Why is that? Think hard.

Is it because, once the message of his boards has registered, you shy away? Is it something more than the simple distraction of the loud lettering on his fore-and-aft screens? When he looks through you with those eyes the colour of shallow winter ponds do you stare back? Or do you look quickly away? Do you? Think — isn't it true? When he walks slowly through the busy mall and his mute messages flash at you, borne as anonymously as radio waves, don't you conspire with him in a game that confers a mutual invisibility?

Because here is the truth; he is invisible, and you see him no more than he sees you. To him, you see, you are just one in a tide of images surging from one smudged plateglass window to the next, your bright colours faded, your existence attenuated. He is paid only to pace, and he paces in a manufactured vacuum. Once, perhaps, he was embarrassed by his trade; if so, he no longer remembers. And as you do not exist, you cannot disturb him now. And think... you, with your delicate susceptibilities, might conceivably feel some embarrassment at the sight of him.

But he is invisible ...

So, you conspire a little.

But conspiracies are fragile. Is it possible that you might falter?

Today might be the day. Test yourself; walk slowly through the wide mall in the bright spring sunshine.

You don't see him? Have patience, don't strain for a glimpse of him, he will be camouflaged by the day's colours. Relax, even executioners must be patient.

There! You see? A sudden break, a slight swirl and jostle up ahead. Walk a little faster.

You see him now, and sudden shock takes you, your stride breaks for a moment. Then you hurry, move closer. And still you cannot believe it until he turns his head a little to the side and you see the pale expressionless face.

For today some terrible metamorphosis has overtaken him; he is clothed, beneath the boards, in a long red dress, glowing scarlet, and on his head is a woman's old black hat, glazed straw, with pink organdie flowers. From below the dress's hem protrude his grey cuffs, his old shoes. But oh, that dress …

His boards are brighter than ever today, daubed with green and orange Dayglo paint … The Paul Sherry All-Male Revue Is Back In Town, they announce, Nitely At Eight, Wine And Dine, Best Show In Town …

After the shock recedes a little, you are puzzled. Did he acquiesce in this barbarity of the dress, the hat? Did he accept the indignity, the ridicule, without demur?

Remember — this morning the world, for him, did not exist.

Watch the faces now as they stream towards him. As always, he walks slowly, making a small eddy in the current of the crowd, so eyes are drawn naturally towards him. Watch the shock, the jar, as the glances lock onto the red vibrance of the dress, the black punctuation of the hat; watch the sudden recognition, apprehension, sly shame, as the eyes move to the placards, rise to the face … then watch them falter, jerk, dart away … away, away, anywhere … into distances, purses, cigarette packets, tree tops, the sudden urgency of trivia.

You cannot see his face, but soon he will reach the end of the pedestrian walk.

See, he is turning now, coming back.

Don't look at his face, watch the placard, wait …

He is nearly here, nearly level …

Now, now! Raise your eyes, fix them on his face. What do you see?

What? You looked away? Dropped a hankie, felt a sudden compulsion to turn and stare into the window behind you?

But it was too late, and you know it. You saw his eyes, saw in them something unfamiliar, saw the first small slow squirmings of a worm called life.

And what did he see in your eyes? What he saw, perhaps, in all the other eyes before they looked away.

So you have a new conspiracy now, you and all the others; you are joined briefly, united in the destruction of his invisibility. You have murdered it with pity, and he knows it.

This afternoon he will leave the streets earlier than usual, take off his boards and stack them neatly, as always, top them with the folded dress, the hat. When he leaves the small room he will not look back, even knowing, as he will, that it is for the last time.

He will walk his usual path, return as always to his small closed rooms. Alone, exposed, he will sit there lacerated by the new raw sensation of life. His nerve ends will jangle, his long thin fingers will tremble a little.

Perhaps, for the first time, he will even look beyond the blind.

You have given him, all of you, a barbed and bitter gift, and he cannot avoid its burden.

The last sandwichman is dead.

An Aim in Life

He was buying it, Vercoe.

But he wasn't using it, as far as I could tell. Of course he could have been sniffing it, or swallowing it, or sticking it up his arse. But as least he wasn't shooting it — there wasn't a tramtrack, a needle-mark, in sight.

And if you knew him you couldn't believe that he was using it, anyway. Apart from anything else he just didn't have the look; he was too open, too regular, too bloody *normal.*

All the same, he was buying.

Vercoe, Vercoe.

High school, the brokers' office. I've known him half my life. Try and picture him: solid, square, blunt-looking; short straight hair, dull blue eyes; and a kind of innocent, earnest quality about him. Something else — an almost indefinable air that hangs about him, seems to cling to him … grey, grey, a greyness …

Yes, that grey thing, an aimlessness, almost a hopelessness.

He's always tried, of course …

You know the kind of guy — tries half-heartedly to play football, cricket, athletics … but never makes the team. Plods along at scholastics … and barely hits the pass mark. Earnest, earnest, one of those terribly earnest ones … but it seems always that they lack some spark, some goad, some goal.

And a kind of amused pity dogs them ... always.

Tolerance.

Bloody cruel, really.

In the end it was strange, though. The way both Vercoe and I ended up working in the same brokers' office. Both of us just cogs, numbers. The great employment lottery. Your number comes up, and there you are. The bright, the dull, the sheep, the goats. Paid the same, valued the same. It's been easy enough for me, but still a tough sweat for Vercoe, with his persistent ... lack.

No drive, they say about him, no aim in life.

But there we were, Vercoe and I, locked among the ledgers, meshed in our clients' accounts — days of contangos and cover notes, slips and bottomry bonds; centre of the city, the city that spawns and sustains us in our thousands. Vercoe and I, I and Vercoe. We are commerce, commerce is us. Vomited out by the indifferent brick halls of our inner-city schools, we are sucked into the great sewer of commerce.

And, every week, Vercoe buys his smack.

He could, I used to think, have a junkie uncle, maybe, auntie, mother — no, not mother; the straitly corseted Mrs Vercoe might get high on aspirin, caffeine, tannin, chocolate éclairs, african violets. But smack would be anathema, horror.

All the same, Vercoe is a buyer.

And right there is a basic paradox: because Vercoe has bought many things. He bought — is buying — a five-acre block down the river (virgin bush, a small creek, a dilapidated shack, no public transport). And each week he buys stamps — prime philatelic investments, guaranteed to appreciate: 40-cent Navigators, 40-cent Primary Industries, 3d Kookaburras, all fine mint. Neatly packaged in glassine bags and enclosed in manila envelopes, they go each week to the bank for safe-keeping. He must have quite a stack by now.

I used to wonder: could *that* be a kind of goal? Early retirement, maybe? Yet Vercoe has never seemed to like the country much.

Anyway, surely, for someone who buys those things … smack seems unthinkable. Those things aren't the purchases of a smack man. Are they?

But still, he went on buying. Smack.

And the mystery remained. What happened to the smack? What did he do with it?

I always knew when he was making a buy: he would begin to avoid me in quite an unusual fashion. A sudden withdrawal, a failure to meet the eye — and Vercoe would slip away to meet a dealer in some sleazy pub. An hour later, when he came back, he would be curiously secretive and sly — quite ludicrous in someone like Vercoe — and a certain tension would permeate his blunt body: Vercoe was carrying.

At those times he was a walking graffito, the apprehension in his bones chalking its mark on the incurious slate of the city — VERCOE BUYS SMACK!

Apart from those surreptitious expeditions Vercoe was almost abnormally normal. He seldom went out with girls — he didn't seem much interested, to tell the truth. He ate sparing lunches. He played a little squash. He watched TV nearly every night.

And each Friday at lunchtime he took his weekly manila envelope to the bank: the week's accumulation of choice philatelic items to add to his hoard. Sometimes I went with him.

Then, one Friday, disaster struck Vercoe. Or at least near disaster; near disaster, near defeat, near disclosure. The injury was the least of it. And for me — ah, for me it was the beginning of some kind of answer, a partial answer, but at least the fulcrum for deeper prying.

I'm afraid I'm rather merciless when my curiosity is roused.

Vercoe's personal disaster was in the shape of a purple EH with mag wheels and what sounded like a V8 motor. As he stepped incautiously off the pavement on his way to the bank with his weekly envelope the EH whipped round the corner, radials squealing, and flung him in the air. He landed flat on the roadway, vehicles screeching aside, plunging away to avoid his prone body. The EH was gone. When I got to him he was conscious; and on his face there was a look — oddly — not of pain or confusion, but of apprehension. I bent over him, saw the sweat breaking out between the runnels of blood and patches of bitumen rash.

He had difficulty moving, but he managed to slip his hand inside his coat. Out came the manila envelope.

'Look after it for me … please!'

There was such a look of abject entreaty on his face that I took it without question and slipped it into my pocket.

Then the ambulance arrived and Vercoe was whipped away — the look of entreaty still unclouded by the obviously mounting pain.

Later I rang the hospital. He was out of danger — bruises and abrasions only, perhaps a mild concussion. A few days in hospital for observation.

Then I remembered the envelope. I took it out of my pocket and had a look at it. Neatly inscribed … 'P.B. Vercoe: for safekeeping'. And at the bottom left-hand corner a pencilled notation of the contents: 1964/65 Birds (blocks of 4), 1965 Anzac 2/3 (10).

Well, who could resist it?

I opened the envelope.

Inside, the stamps were neatly packed in their glassine envelopes and taped to a piece of card. And also taped to the card were four small packets of white powder.

Well, if you want to keep heroin there's no safer place than a bank, I suppose.

All the same, Vercoe had some questions to answer.

Pale and bandaged, Vercoe looked as much a stranger in the hospital ward as he did in the rest of the world. There were half a dozen beds in the ward, all occupied, all surrounded by visitors. Except Vercoe's. And all the visitors seemed intent on talking at once. Loudly. Strange, hospital visitors always seem to feel that their sick victims are struck with deafness along with their other infirmities. Thus, noise. And the man in the bed next to Vercoe had suffered a recent stroke and moaned loudly most of the time. So Vercoe and I occupied a small island of privacy in the aviary of the ward.

He was pretty stiff and sore, Vercoe, and couldn't move much. And he had to lie flat. But he could talk. In a kind of strange, strained whisper. But he *could* talk. I filled a few minutes with callous platitudes; increasing his tensions, softening him up. That way confession might come a little easier. I kept the talk to all kinds of nothing things. But I couldn't wait too long. His mother might arrive at any moment.

But before that happened Vercoe broke.

'You've got the envelope?' His voice was low and strained.

'Envelope?' I frowned. 'What ... oh, that envelope. Yeah, I've got it somewhere ...'

'Somewhere!'

Well, a joke's a joke, but enough's enough. I leaned forward and spoke close to his ear. 'What the hell are you doing with that smack?'

'You opened it!'

I grinned at him. 'Going to tell me about it?'

He was silent for a long time. When finally he spoke he sounded more serious, more ... I don't know, resolute ... than I'd ever heard him before. 'I've got this block up the river ...'

I was a bit nonplussed. 'Yeah ...'

'I'm going to retire there in a few years ...'

I began to wonder if he was delirious. That crack on the head ...'

'Listen,' he said, 'you know I've never been ... well, I've never fitted in. I've never been any *good* at anything ... nothing that mattered ... nothing in life that *really* mattered ... and I've never had anything that ... really *grabbed* me ... nothing to look forward to ... nothing ... *you* know ...'

The understatement of the year. The biggest thing in Vercoe's life was probably coming in ninth in the school cross-country.

'What's that got to do with it?'

'Remember,' he said, 'when they took the cartilage out ... in the hospital ... the first day after the operation it hurt like buggery. They came along and asked me if I wanted something for the pain. I said, yes, I did. It was bloody awful ...'

I really couldn't imagine what the hell he was on about.

'They gave me a shot of morphine,' he said, and lay there, colourless and pathetic, but somehow relaxed, as if it was all over, as if he'd explained everything.

I looked blank. I waited.

But he just lay there looking up at me as if he'd finally explained everything, bared his soul. The catharsis of confession. Except that he didn't seem to have confessed anything.

'Don't you understand?' he said. 'That shot — it was just like being pulled suddenly into heaven ... a glorious floating painless limbo ... not just the pain gone, but all the awfulness of life, too ... all the shrivelling embarrassments, all the shit I'd ever taken, all the crap I'd ever had to swallow ... all the emptiness, the aimlessness ... all gone ... all that was left was this glorious painless euphoria ... it was better than *anything* I'd ever known ... *anything*.' He paused. 'And anything I've ever had since ...'

'Don't tell me you got hooked on one shot of morphine?'

He shook his head painfully, and a little scornfully. 'Nothing like that. It was just that ... thinking about it later ... it was the beginning ... the beginning of some sort of conscious decision ... everything I've done since then ... it's all been aimed at ...'

'Aimed at what?'

'I'm going to be a junkie ... as soon as I can afford it ...'

'What!'

He sighed. 'You know what I've always been like ... nothing's ever worked out for me ... never any real life, nothing ... just a kind of grey filling-in time till I die. It's been different for you ...'

'Jesus, man, that's just self-pity!'

'No, not really. The truth is ... I'm just nothing,' He paused. 'But that other ... that shot of morphine ... it really *was* something ... a glimpse of colour, of life, what it *could* be like for me.' He reached out and gripped my hand. 'Don't you understand? It's bloody paradise! And I can *have* it! *Years* of it!'

'Christ, heroin! It'll kill you ...'

'I know,' he said, 'but they reckon it takes at least five years. If you were like me, wouldn't you trade the rest of your life for five years of paradise? Just think ... I'll have enough money, enough smack, I won't have to work to support a habit ... all the junk I need ... I'll just move up to my shack ... and go to heaven.'

'What happens at the end?' I didn't know whether to laugh or cry. Vercoe with an aim in life!'

He moved his shoulders a little, wincing. 'If I run out of stuff before the end I'll just OD ...'

He grabbed my arm again, his face anxious below the bandages. 'Listen, you won't tell, will you? Promise?'

Of course, I promised.

When I left he was lying back against the pillows,

colourless again and lost in the noisy tide of the ward, dreaming already I suppose of the endless nirvana of life at his shack … smack, morning, noon and night.

Vercoe's aim in life. Christ!

I kept my promise. What else could I do, anyway? Who am I to deny him? I tell myself, anyway, that maybe he won't go through with it, that maybe he'll meet a nice girl and settle down, that maybe … but I know deep down, of course, that he *will* do it. The truth is, there just isn't anything else for him now; now he knows it's there. I know him well enough to know he won't change.

He's back at work now, no ill effects from the accident.

And buying smack again.

Going to the bank every Friday with his manila envelope.

There's a difference now, though. When he goes off to buy his smack he no longer avoids my eye. We have a secret now — you could say even that we're conspirators.

And sometimes I have a strange feeling that Vercoe is laughing at us, at all of us.

Shells

He waited under the trees where the shadows latticed the yellow light from the streetlamps; a thin Chinese, neither tall nor short, old or young. His hair was dark and thick, cut short, his face lined a little about mouth and eye-corners. He was watching the doorway of the Club Pitate across the road. It was 1 o'clock, and behind him at the end of the yacht harbour the black bulk of La Jonque was shuttered, closed for the night, its dragon-bright scarlet trim no more than a faint lacquered sheen. A small wind stirred the branches of the trees, the moving leaves trailing their shadows gently over him.

An occasional car cruised the Boulevard Pomare behind the moving iodine yellow of its headlights. But the doorway across the road continued to hold his attention, as it had for the past hour.

He had followed them along the Boulevard from the Whisky-A-Go-Go, a nondescript and silent figure in his dark blue slacks and shirt, drifting unnoticed in the wake of the small raucous cluster of youths. They had disappeared into the club, had been engulfed, were concealed now somewhere behind the windows that glowed warm and rosy-pink in the warm night. The open doorway framed darkness and the stir of undefined movement, a sense of quietly seething bodies just beyond the limits of vision. The music from the club was very loud, and seemed to take on an almost physical weight, flooding from the sounding-boards of the curtained glass, spilling from the doorway, rolling across the clutter of parked motor cycles, beating across the empty street, losing itself at last over the quiet waters of Papeete Roads.

In the nebulous shadows of the club doorway new shadows moved, found slow definition, and three figures appeared suddenly in relief against the darkness, stepped out into the street. Two of them were men, the other a girl.

For a moment or two the group was held together by the thin string of muttered conversation. Then the girl hooked her arm in the arm of one of the men, drew him away. They moved southward, towards the darker streets. The remaining man stood alone, swaying a little, seeming uncertain.

The Chinese crossed the street quickly, his crêpe-soled shoes making almost no sound on the soft tarmac.

The man — he seemed in the pool of the streetlamp little more than a boy — saw the Chinese approaching. He peered, with strange turtle-like weavings of his head, into the roadway.

'Lee? Lee, is that you?' He was very drunk, and the small dark moustache seemed oddly artificial, almost as if pasted on the waxy sheen of his sallow face. His close-set brown eyes were unfocused and vague.

'Come on,' said Lee, 'let's get you off the Boulevard.' He took the boy's arm.

The boy braced his feet, held his ground. He blinked, but said nothing.

'Come on, Gérard, they'll pick you up for certain.' The patrol wagon was stationed usually at the north end of the Quai du Commerce, but often it cruised the lighted streets.

The boy slumped a little, allowed himself to follow the pressure of the guiding arm. 'Where are we going?'

'Wherever you like … anywhere, as long as it's off the streets.'

The boy stopped again, dragging the Chinese to a halt. 'But where, then?' he persisted.

'My place if you like.'

'No,' said Gérard, 'not there, not your place.'

'You can't go back to the base like this.'

'No.'

'All right. Come on.' He led the boy round the corner inton the Avenue Bruat, guided him for several blocks until they came to his old white rust-ridden Citroen. He held open the passenger's door and the boy slumped wordlessly into the seat, lay back, closed his eyes.

Lee drove eastward, swung onto the Rue Colette. Passing the long iron roofs of the markets in the Rue Cardella, the sweet sappy pungency of pineapples drifted through the open windows of the car. He turned north, driving out of the city. There was little traffic. Gérard was silent until they were passing through the heavy suburban silence of Arue.

'I feel ill,' he said then, apologetically.

Lee pulled the car to the side of the road, stopped. Gérard opened the door, began to get out. But halfway through the door he paused, vomited suddenly onto the roadway. In a moment he slumped back into the car. 'I'm all right now. I'm sorry ...'

Lee turned his head, looked at him. 'Wipe your mouth,' he said, handing the boy a tissue. 'And your shoe.' He let in the clutch and steered carefully from the kerb, avoiding the pool of vomit.

'Where are we going?'

'Pointe Vénus. Unless you want to go somewhere else ...?'

'No ... that's all right.'

Lee took the turnoff that led back towards the sea.

They sat silently for a little on the steps of the small

museum, between the two ancient pitted cannons. The point was deserted, the car-park empty, the kiosk shuttered. Between the boles of the tall palms the white finger of the lighthouse probed the dark sky. There was a faint breeze that rattled the fronds. The sea was as dark as the sky, murmuring distantly, softly.

'I've been drinking cognac,' said Gérard. 'I shouldn't, I know, it always makes me ill.' He was recovering a little now, almost sober, but his face still shone a little in the faint light with the sweat of passing nausea.

'Never mind,' said Lee, lighting another cigarette. 'Never mind …'

After a little Gérard said, 'I want to lie down for a bit…'

They walked slowly along the deserted paths towards the beach. On the coarse black sand they sat side by side looking out across the quiet water towards the shelving hills, the faint outline of the mountains, the thin prickling of lights. Gérard lay back, cradling his head on his locked palms.

'What time do you have to be back on base?' asked Lee.

'It doesn't matter,' said Gérard. 'About seven. They won't worry too much on the last day.'

'No.'

And they were both silent again.

After a time the boy turned on his side, his back to Lee, cradled his cheek in his palms, and slept.

At the bottom of the steep slope of the beach the water lapped softly at the dark sand. The stars moved with slow precision across the blank face of the sky. Lee smoked almost continuously, and, a little after three, went back to the car for more cigarettes. When he returned he saw that the boy was still sleeping. For a moment he stood motionless in the deep shadow of a tall ironwood, watching the motionless figure on the beach. The white shirt, the blur of the face, were pale, almost luminous in the night. He lit another cigarette and sat down again beside the boy.

Half his pack of cigarettes was gone, the butts littering the sand, before a faint greyness edged at the sky behind them. The beach itself seemed in darker shadow than ever. He looked at his watch. Four-thirty. He stubbed out his cigarette, screwed the butt deeply, almost violently, into the sand; leaned over, and with the back of a gentle forefinger, traced the smooth line of the sleeping boy's cheek.

'It's time, *mon cher* ...'

Lee parked the car a block from his fabric shop, and they walked across the road to the Café Roti. They sat at one of the small tables that lined the walls. Outside it was growing light, and in the street outside traffic was beginning to thunder down towards the centre of the city; cars, motorbikes, vans, *les trucks* gaudy in red and blue and green with their transistors blaring, carrying their cargoes of early workers, ladders, coconuts; yams, pineapples, baskets, bundles.

A thin girl placed rolls and large cups of strong black coffee on their table. Around them workers and their families were taking their breakfasts.

'What time do you leave?' asked Lee. 'Tonight?'

'Nine-thirty,' said Gérard, his face buried in his cup. He looked tired and ill. 'We have to be there an hour early.'

'Can I pick you up?'

'No, I have to go out with the others.'

'Well, then, I'll see you at the airport.'

'All right.' Gérard would not look at him.

'I'll have to go soon,' said Lee. 'The shop ...'

'Yes.'

After a long pause Lee spoke again. 'I've been thinking — I haven't had a holiday in years. I might take a trip to France. I've never been there ...' His voice was suddenly hesitant, less certain, less composed. 'I can afford it, after all. Why shouldn't I?'

Gérard said nothing.

'I might even come to Lyons. I could see you then, couldn't I? You'll be working there, won't you?'

'I suppose so ...'

The ambiguity of his answer hung in the air between them. Lee bit his lip, stared out through the wide doorway at the railed park, the tall pandanus trees buttressed with their stilted roots, the flags and neat paintwork of the *Mairie* across the Rue Paul Gauguin. 'I'll have to go,' he said.

Gérard nodded.

'Will I get a taxi for you?'

'No,' said Gérard, 'don't wait. I'll finish my coffee, then I'll find one ...'

'All right,' said Lee. He stood up. 'Well, tonight, then ...'

'Yes, all right ...'

Lee walked out into the street without looking back. In the new grey light of the morning he seemed suddenly much too slight, too fragile a figure to be facing the rushing weight of the day.

Lee drove slowly through the deepening dusk into the carpark at Faaa, parked carefully opposite the main entrance to the terminal. He was early, far too early, and he sat for a few minutes watching the glow of the yellow lights from the great thatched market, the wide circle of idle shell-sellers, their mounds of necklaces, still covered with strips of bright pareu print.

He looked down at the pile of shell leis on the seat beside him. They had been bought that afternoon at one of the city stalls. He left them where they lay, got out, locked the car, and walked across the road into the terminal. It was almost deserted; he could see only a few porters and a cluster of drinkers about the ground-floor bar. His footsteps echoed dully on the yellow tiles. He climbed the stairs to the long balcony. Apart from a cluster of small planes near the Air Polynésie terminal the only aircraft in sight was the white DC8 with the tricolour on the tail and the République de France banner on its fuselage.

The night was warm, still, clear. The faintest edge of pink touched the tops of Moorea's peaks ten miles away across the sea.

He went into the bar at the end of the balcony, ordered a pastis, sat at a table.

The only other customer was a pot-bellied French *sous-officier* drinking Heineken at the counter.

Sipping his drink slowly, chain-smoking, he glanced at his watch every few minutes. Finally, at ten minutes to eight, he stood up and went out onto the landing. Several young men in slacks and shirts brushed past him on their way up. He started down the stairs.

On the bottom flight the rising tide of noise met him and, as the concourse came into sight, he stopped for a moment.

What had been, thirty minutes before, a deserted and echoing cavern was now a seething hive, crammed with jostling milling bodies. The shuffling clatter of feet, the hum of febrile last-minute conversations, rose and hung in the high spaces of the building with all the weighty palpability of a locust cloud. Lee took a deep breath and went on down.

He pushed his way slowly through the crowd; it was composed mostly of young men. All of them wore civilian dress — mostly neat shirts and sober slacks. Many had shell leis about their necks. Here and there an ungarlanded youth would seize another firmly, kiss him briefly on both cheeks. The faces of those with shell necklaces seemed fixed in a smiling vacuity, a kind of euphoria that promised to hold them well into the night, well into their long flight home.

He could not see Gérard.

At the entrance all the booths — except for the military one — were deserted. Close by stood a bored French sergeant, plump and dark, and four lounging Tahitian military policemen in white helmets, swinging their black batons. Lee went past them, crossed the road to the carpark. It was crowded now. He unlocked his car, took out the shell leis and turned back to the terminal. By now the vendors in the rotunda were doing brisk business, the market was crowded, and the piles of leis were shrinking.

Inside the building again, lost in the throng, Lee stood for a moment, the crowd eddying about him. Under the noise and bustle it was all in fact quite orderly. There was little drunkenness, merely a kind of feverish and sustained excitement. The MPs looked bored. Here and there a few family groups stood anchored in the currents of the crowd: older men with wives and children; officers, NCOs, completing another tour of duty, going home to metropolitan France to wait for a new posting. But for the most part the concourse was packed with the boys, finished with Tahiti, free — or almost free — after their two years in uniform. There were few women in the crowd; only a scattering of laughing Polynesian tarts.

Lee moved to the stairs again to find a better view. It was some minutes before he saw Gérard.

He was standing with a group of his friends by the gift shop. The drunken pallor of the morning was gone and he looked tanned and healthy. And very young. The ridiculous moustache seemed to weigh down his boy's face with a ridiculous gravity. Already he wore several strands of shells round his neck.

Lee approached the group slowly, hesitated a few paces away.

One of the young men noticed him, nudged Gérard slyly. The boy turned, caught sight of Lee, smiled a little uncertainly, waved a hand.

Lee waited.

At last Gérard detached himself from the group, came and stood beside him, saying nothing.

'You're all right, then?' said Lee.

'Of course.'

They stood in awkward silence.

'Here,' said Lee suddenly. 'These are for you ...' Quickly he draped the leis round Gérard's neck, piling them on those already there.

'Oh ... thank you.'

Silence claimed them again.

'What time do you have to board?' asked Lee at last.

'Oh,' said Gérard, 'soon, I guess. They've started already.'

'What ...!' Turning, Lee saw that there was a small queue at the door of the security area. He looked at his watch. Eight-fifteen. He looked back at Gérard, his lips twisting into a sick rictal smile that edged towards panic. He touched Gérard lightly on the arm. 'Perhaps next year ... I'll come to France. Maybe I'll see you then?'

Gérard said nothing. Lee closed his eyes for a moment.

A group pressed past them, moving to join the queue. One of the men wore a collar of shells so high that he could hardly turn his head.

'I must get you more leis,' said Lee suddenly, desperately. 'You haven't enough, you must have more. Wait for me ... please?' And he was gone, dodging through the crowd, across the road into the rotunda. He seized a great armful of leis from the nearest table, thrust a sheaf of notes at the old woman.

Inside the terminal the crowd seemed to have coagulated about the security door. From twenty paces away he could see that Gérard was at the head of the queue.

'Gérard!'

But the glass door had opened, and Gérard was gone.

Lee pushed his way to the glass wall, pressed his face close to the smudged pane. Gérard was hefting his small suitcase onto the inspection counter. Lee saw his mouth open, the words lost beyond the heavy glass, as he exchanged a joke with the two blue-uniformed officers. Then he walked quickly through the metal-detector, picked up his case, waved once — to the security officers — and was gone.

Upstairs people were gathering on the balcony, peering down at the trickle of passengers walking towards the floodlit plane. Lee watched for half an hour, but he did not see Gérard.

Then, very quickly it seemed, the last passenger had boarded, the doors were closed, and the ramp driven off. The engines began to whine with mounting power. Lee looked around him then. There was a scattering of people left on the balcony: a few boys, a gaggle of laughing Poly-nesian girls, the bored French sergeant, the four MPs leaning against a wall, joking, smiling, tapping each other's helmets with their batons. In none of the faces was there any trace of pain, of sadness, of loss.

The plane began to taxi away, its red navigation lights flashing.

Lee was suddenly aware of the weight of the redundant leis.

The great white plane roared distantly, then thundered suddenly out of the darkness. It lifted, and was lost to sight for a moment behind the end of the building. Then it reap-peared, impossibly high, a tiny cluster of red stars, growing rapidly smaller, climbing over Pointe Vénus and out into the empty ocean that curved away towards Los Angeles.

Downstairs the concourse was almost empty. Lee dumped the bundle of leis on the counter of the empty Avis booth, the shells rattling emptily on the bare laminex.

As he unlocked the door of his old Citroen Lee could see that the shell-sellers were covering their tables again, settling under their wraps to wait for the next plane. The night had a faintly sickly smell of crushed frangipani and dust and burnt jet fuel.